Coffee Break

"Kinda outta your jurisdiction—ain't ya, Long?"

Longarm sipped his coffee and nodded. "One of the men they killed with the Silverjack wagon—the one-legged jehu—was a friend of mine." He ran his tongue across his front teeth, containing his rage. "A very good friend I hadn't seen in a while."

"That's a shame." The curly-haired gent lowered his chin slightly and rolled his eyes to regard the big man furtively. Sweat shone on his red brown forehead. "Reckon you won't get to see him at all again now."

Sucking a sharp breath, he worried his boot toe against the rock again and said, "So, these killers . . . you run any of 'em down yet?"

Longarm had just sipped his coffee. He held it in his mouth for a moment, then swallowed it with a faint gurgling sound as he stared up from beneath his mantled brows at the two men sitting across the fire. "Just you two . . ."

It happened so fast that Longarm wasn't even sure which man he'd shot first before the flicker of movement across the fire caught his eye, and with an automatic movement driven more by instinct than thought, his double-action Colt was leaping and roaring in his hand.

TABOR EVANS

LONGARM

AND THE GUN TRAIL

JOVE BOOKS, NEW YORK

THE BERKLEY PUBLISHING GROUP
Published by the Penguin Group
Penguin Group (USA) Inc.
375 Hudson Street, New York, New York 10014, USA
Penguin Group (Canada), 90 Eglinton Avenue East, Suite 700, Toronto, Ontario M4P 2Y3, Canada
(a division of Pearson Penguin Canada Inc.)
Penguin Books Ltd., 80 Strand, London WC2R 0RL, England
Penguin Group Ireland, 25 St. Stephen's Green, Dublin 2, Ireland (a division of Penguin Books Ltd.)
Penguin Group (Australia), 250 Camberwell Road, Camberwell, Victoria 3124, Australia
(a division of Pearson Australia Group Pty. Ltd.)
Penguin Books India Pvt. Ltd., 11 Community Centre, Panchsheel Park, New Delhi—110 017, India
Penguin Group (NZ), 67 Apollo Drive, Rosedale, North Shore 0632, New Zealand
(a division of Pearson New Zealand Ltd.)
Penguin Books (South Africa) (Pty.) Ltd., 24 Sturdee Avenue, Rosebank, Johannesburg 2196,
South Africa

Penguin Books Ltd., Registered Offices: 80 Strand, London WC2R 0RL, England

This is a work of fiction. Names, characters, places, and incidents either are the product of the author's imagination or are used fictitiously, and any resemblance to actual persons, living or dead, business establishments, events, or locales is entirely coincidental.

LONGARM AND THE GUN TRAIL

A Jove Book / published by arrangement with the author

PRINTING HISTORY
Jove edition / July 2009

Copyright © 2009 by Penguin Group (USA) Inc.
Cover illustration by Miro Sinovcic.

ISBN: 978-0-515-14651-6

JOVE®
Jove Books are published by The Berkley Publishing Group,
a division of Penguin Group (USA) Inc.,
375 Hudson Street, New York, New York 10014.
JOVE® is a registered trademark of Penguin Group (USA) Inc.
The "J" design is a trademark of Penguin Group (USA) Inc.

PRINTED IN THE UNITED STATES OF AMERICA

10 9 8 7 6 5 4 3 2 1

Chapter 1

The incomparable Miss Cynthia Larimer glanced around her painter's easel, pooched out her delectable, bee-stung lips, and beseeched with a frustrated frown, "Cus-tisss, won't you please take off that *beastly* hat?"

"No."

"It's ruining the effect."

"The effect of what?"

"Of my *plein air*, of course," she said with a snit, her gauzy flowered wrap blowing out around her naked shoulders. She wore nothing under the unbuttoned wrap, and Longarm craned his head to get a gander at those incredible breasts partly hidden by her easel and shaded by her straw picture hat, from which silk ribbons fluttered in the warm summer breeze.

"What's plain air again?" he asked. "I forget."

"*Plein air*," Cynthia enunciated in French. She sighed with strained patience, and dabbed her brush at the canvas propped on the easel before her. "It's painting while outside, moron. Now, please remove the hat. I want to paint you entirely nude, not so much as a blade of grass obscuring that big, brown, manly carcass of yours!"

Longarm glanced at his clothes piled on a flat rock, his low-heeled cavalry boots set beneath them. He rolled his eyes down his broad, naked chest and flat belly to his snuff brown hat, which he clutched to his groin with one hand draped across his naked hip as he lounged in the grass.

He puffed the nickel cheroot between his lips and narrowed an eye at the girl, who sat behind her easel with her long, coltish legs crossed—pale and smooth as freshly polished marble—as she leaned forward to concentrate. Her feet, one buried in the green timothy, the toes of the other lightly brushing the grass blades, were long and delicate, perfectly formed.

As was the rest of her, right up to each strand of her long, raven black hair.

"Uh-uh," he said, letting smoke trickle out around his cigar. "I'm, uh . . . in season, so to speak. I don't want you paintin' me with no hard-on, then showin' it around to your European friends so you can laugh and make fun of the randy Western lawdog."

Cynthia giggled and stared over the top of her canvas, holding her brush out beside her. "Show me."

Longarm shook his head. "You'll paint it."

"None of my friends in Europe know you from Adam's off ox, Custis. And as promised, I'm obscuring your face. Now, please remove the hat and let me finish the painting so we can chill our wine in the creek and dig into our picnic basket."

"No food till I do?"

"No food till you do."

Longarm grumbled a curse. He didn't know how in the

hell he'd let himself be talked into letting the girl paint him in the raw in the first place. He glanced at her full, round breasts again, jostling between the open flaps of the gauzy wrap.

Well . . . maybe he did know. And as long as he'd let her get this far . . .

He removed the hat and tossed it into the grass behind him. His long, thick dong jutted out from his crotch, the purple mushroom head swollen and bobbing slightly with each lusty heartbeat.

"Is that for me, Custis?" she said, staring over the canvas in admiration, tightening her crossed, bare legs slightly, and squirming around on the rock she used for a stool.

"Any other pretty, naked girls out here?" He frowned and looked away, puffing his cigar and feeling his ears warm. "Come on, Cynthia—finish up. What if someone comes along?"

Smiling and continuing to squirm, shaking her crossed leg and flexing her toes, she shuttled her studious, cobalt gaze from his rigid cock to her canvas and back again, her right elbow jostling as she painted. A smile grew slowly on her long, red mouth. Finally, she pulled her arm back from the canvas.

"Done!" She swept her gaze once more along his horsey brown frame lounging in the green, breeze-brushed grass. "And, if I do say, I think I've captured your likeness rather well. My teachers in Paris will be pleased."

She dabbed at her brush with a rag and uncoiled from her rock like a long, beautiful, curvaceous cat. She dropped the canvas covering over the picture, then strode toward Longarm, naked as the day she was born despite the over-sized hat and the sheer, flowered wrap that blew out behind her shoulders in the wind, deliciously revealing every inch of her pale, willowy body—from jostling, pink-tipped breasts to the V of silky black hair between her smooth-muscled thighs.

"Got any wood to split with this ax?" she said, kneeling beside him, grabbing his rock-hard cock with one hand, wrapping her other arm around his neck, and closing her open mouth over his.

She gently pumped him a couple of times, pulling the skin up above the head of his dong, then splayed her fingers over his scrotum, hefting his balls. "Custus . . ." she whispered as she nuzzled his ear. "Why is it that I'll travel thousands of miles over and over again in a year just to be with you a week at a time?"

"I think we both know the answer to that one, darlin'," Longarm said, sitting up and gentling her straight back down onto the grass.

Her hat blew off her head; she let it go. Her hair lifted like ravens' wings. Her wrapper blew open, revealing her in all her creamy beauty. One at a time, Longarm lifted her legs over his shoulders, caressing her thighs with his big, brown hands, then lowered his head to her snatch, sniffing and nuzzling her hungrily, like a coyote that hadn't fed for days.

"Custis!" she cried with a start, closing her hands over his head and brusquely pulling his hair as he worked expertly between her spread thighs. She rolled her head from side to side, groaning and grunting, eyes snapping wide in erotic euphoria. "Oh . . . Jesus . . . God . . . you know just . . . how to do me, don't you, you *bastard*!"

He slid his mustached lips and tongue up and down her slit, grinning as she gave all the expected reactions to his manipulations, which had been learned over the two years since they'd met in Denver. When he had her fairly sobbing and soaked, her belly shuddering beneath his forehead, he drew back onto his knees. Breathing heavily, he rose and extended his hands to her.

"Time to get down to brass tacks."

"Oh . . . Jesus . . . what . . . ?"

She tossed a weak hand up. He grabbed it and drew her to her feet. In his lust-crazed state, she seemed to weigh no more than a feather pillow. When he had her standing, swooning, before him, he bent his knees and wrapped his hands under the backsides of her thighs. He lifted her up to his waist, holding her out before him, then settling her gently, slowly down onto his cock, which was as hard as the central drive shaft on a Baldwin locomotive.

He stretched his lips back from his teeth and sucked a sharp breath of exquisite pain, feeling the muscles down his back ripple sweetly.

She gasped and pressed her hands against both sides of his head, drawing him to her and closing her ripe, wet lips over his, shoving her tongue as far back into his mouth as it would go, waggling it around desperately. Her mouth always tasted like cherries. As he turned and pushed her up and down on his burning organ, she locked her ankles behind his back.

Then he bent his knees and slowly, fluidly lowered her back down to the grass already flattened by his own body, letting her head rest gently against the ground. Then he rose up on outstretched arms and began thrusting wildly, grunting and groaning madly between her legs, which he held up and back to nearly her ears.

As he toiled furiously, she ground her fingers into his bulging, dark-red biceps and occasionally lifted her lips to his, nibbling him and entangling her tongue with his before flopping her head back down to the grass and sobbing and laughing in a nether region of carnal ravishment and drunken bliss.

They'd done this dance so many times before that she could tell when he was about to erupt.

"No!" she cried, fairly sobbing and pounding his shoulders with her fists. "Wait!"

Longarm stopped thrusting and looked at the girl, incredulous. *"Huh?"*

"Get off!"

"What?"

She finally got him to roll over onto his hip and shoulder, looking at her as though she'd just grown an extra head. Grunting and groaning as though in a deadly tussle with a rogue grizzly, she shoved him onto his back and then straddled him . . . backward.

Longarm lifted his head to look at her slender back as she lifted her pretty, round ass and dropped her chin to see the workings down below. At the same time she grabbed his cock in her right fist—he was so close to explosion that the pressure of her warm hand nearly did it—and held him straight up and down while she slowly lowered her bottom.

"Jay-zuz," he groaned as her sopping snatch, heated to near boiling, slid slowly down over his shaft.

"Oh!" she cried, propped on her arms and using her knees to raise and lower her bottom.

She worked slowly at first, her entire body quivering, digging her fingers into his knees.

Cunning and purposeful in her lovemaking, Cynthia slowly built momentum, her bottom rising and falling, rising and falling with more speed and fury, until it made slapping sounds against his belly, until it walloped him nearly senseless and he could hear the crackling of their mingling fluids.

Her hair bounced down her back—so long it tickled his chest. Her ass became a pale blur beneath it. Her cries were like the savage screams of an Apache squaw hacking apart what was left of dying federal soldiers.

She increased her speed even more . . . until her silky, wet, pistoning snatch lifted him to such heights of carnal bliss that he set his jaws and tore at the grass beside him, yearning for surcease while at the same time wishing the otherworldly torture would last forever but kill him just a little every eon.

Finally, his metaphorical thumb couldn't hold the flood waters back any longer. He'd become hopelessly lost in his backward recitation of the books in the Old Testament. With a snarling bellow and enraged baring of his teeth and hardening of his jaws, he lifted his head, grabbed the girl around her slender waist, and pulled her down toward him while he arched his back and thrust his hips straight up against her.

His bellow and her scream mingled as he exploded inside her—so far up, it felt, that he could feel the pounding of her heart against the head of his leaping, spasming cock.

Her bottom wiggled and shook for a long time.

Then, gradually, seemingly one by one, the muscles in her back relaxed and she let her rump slide back down atop his now-spent and dwindling dong as she faced his feet.

She laughed giddily. She reached up, ran her hands slowly, luxuriously through her mussed hair, then let it fall back down to caress his chest.

She sighed, long and slow, so that it sounded like a cat's mewl. "Jesus, you fuck good, Custis."

"Seems to me you did most of the—"

"Oh, God," she said sharply, cutting him off, stiffening suddenly.

"What?"

"Oh, *no!*"

Blinking as though awakening from a long nap, Longarm pushed up on his elbows and cast his gaze over one of the girl's delicate shoulders.

Several horseback riders and a buggy drawn by a single, white horse had just crested a distant ridge, the snow-mantled peaks of western Colorado's Sawatch Range looming high and broad behind them. They followed a two-track trail down off the ridge and around an aspen copse as they angled toward Longarm and Miss Cynthia—150 yards away and closing.

"Is that who it looks like?" Longarm croaked.

"If you think it looks like my dear uncle, General Larimer himself, with Aunt May beside him—it *is!*"

Cynthia had already lurched up from her perch on Longarm's sleeping member and dashed off to gather her clothes.

"Quick, Custis!" The girl's breathless voice trembled as she tossed his hat onto his crotch, then reached for her pantaloons and one delicate green shoe. "If the general and my pious aunt find us stark naked and spent from fucking like two crazy minks, we're wolf bait!"

Chapter 2

General William H. Larimer III was considered by most to be Denver's founding father. Counties, towns, streets, and babies were named after him. He was the wealthiest man in Colorado Territory as well as the one with the most political power. No Denver mayor or Colorado territorial governor had ever taken office without his political blessing.

He was also a deeply religious man. A man who loved his beautiful niece, Cynthia, born with a silver spoon firmly fixed between those exquisite blow job lips, with all his pious heart. Having been cursed with two daughters who were not only fat and ugly, but dull and stupid and owning no appreciation at all for the fine arts or world travel, the general prized his raven-haired niece nearly as much as the blooded Thoroughbreds and Tennessee trotters dwelling better than his servants in the lavish stables flanking his mansion on Denver's exclusive Sherman Avenue.

Longarm was almost as afraid of what might happen to the general himself if he discovered that his niece had been fornicating, not only with a male from the lowly working

classes, but with a lawman who hailed from the humblest
of humble backgrounds. The general would surely have
Longarm fired, and barred from working anywhere again
but in livery barns, forking shit from horse and mule stalls
for pennies and piss water and an occasional nickel cheroot.
He might also terminate Longarm's supervisor, Chief Marshal Billy Vail of the First District Court of Colorado, if he
didn't incur a heart stroke or brain stroke first.

Dear, sweet, plump Aunt May would be shocked out of
her senses, and probably spend the rest of her days screaming and tearing her gray hair out in some Gothic-spired
insane asylum overlooking the pounding Atlantic on the
rocky coast of Maine.

As for Cynthia—well, her own immediate family had
plenty of money, but she'd doubtless be barred from setting
foot not only in Denver, but probably anywhere west of the
Mississippi ever again . . . which meant her and Longarm's
hog-wallowing stark-naked wrestling matches, limbs and
tongues entwined, would be over and done with.

Or so it seemed at the moment anyway, so soon after
fucking the horny vixen. The rattle of the general's wagon
grew louder as Longarm and Cynthia scrambled around,
throwing their clothes on, the crack of the general's whip
sounding like sporadic pistol fire just beyond the knoll they
crouched behind.

"Do you think they saw us?" Cynthia said, still breathless, eyes sharp with fright, as she lowered her lacy, pink,
low-cut summer frock down over her porcelain-pale willowy frame. She had no time to don any of the ten pounds
of silk or cotton underwear that were part and parcel of
being a female in the late Victorian Era.

She glanced around the shoulder of the knoll, as did
Longarm, who'd sat on a rock to pull on a cavalry boot. The

wagon was just now emerging from the breeze-tussled aspens forty yards away.

"When they were at the top of the ridge," Cynthia continued, turning to hide her underwear behind Longarm's rock and weighing it down with a stone, "they had a clear shot at us."

"Don't say 'shot,'" Longarm said with a wince as his boot slapped against his heel. "I hear the general's blind as a bat. How's Miss May's vision these days?"

"Does it matter?" Cynthia hissed, straightening and smoothing her dress, peering down her bosom to make sure all was relatively in order. "Even if the general or Aunt May didn't see us both stark naked, their bodyguards must have! Oh, Custis, what are we gonna do?"

"I have my Colt .44," the lawman said. "We could commit double suicide before they get here, and win their sympathy. But then they'd likely see your plain air canvas with my dong at full red mast, and bury us in one of them paupers' trenches on the low-rent side of Cherry Creek."

"This is no time for jokes, you rogue."

"Who's joking?" Longarm slapped her rump as she started out from behind the knoll, adding in a low whisper, "At least we'd be handy when we got randy!"

The Larimers' leather-seated, tassle-canopied carriage pulled up near Cynthia's easel, the ribald painting itself, however, safely cloaked behind a canvas cover. The general and Mrs. Larimer were looking around as though lost, the general himself holding the white horse's ribbons, until Cynthia said, "Uncle! Aunty! What on earth are you doing way out here?"

Her voice teemed with false cheer, and Longarm, plucking a nickel cheroot from the breast pocket of his pinstriped shirt, noted a nervous quaver.

"Cynthia, dear!" intoned the buxom Aunt May. "I thought I spied you down here before William drove us into the trees!"

"How are you, my dear?" the general asked from behind his dusty, round, silver-rimmed spectacles. He was dressed in his usual army parade-grade blues, complete with cavalry sword, although Longarm wasn't sure that he'd ever fought in any wars, including the Indian Wars, though the moneyed gent inferred frequently that he had. "Thought we'd spied you down here, but couldn't be sure. Saw the easel, though. Painting, are we?"

"Oh, yes." Cynthia beamed nervously and rose up on her toes, holding her arms close to her sides to conceal the fact she wasn't wearing any underwear. "What a place to appreciate the flora and fauna. I'm so glad we decided to vacation in the Rockies. Custis and I were just running down a . . . uh"—she slid her edgy gaze to Longarm as if looking for help—"a blue-winged warbler when we heard you approach. I haven't painted one of those yet. Plenty of hummingbirds and camp robber jays, but no warblers of any stripe!"

One of the three bodyguards—all beefy, mustached gents dressed in black suits with string ties and crisp bowler hats—pinched his hat brim at Cynthia and asked, "What were you painting, Miss Cynthia?" The man, whose name was Reed Salvitch, gave Longarm a devilish glance. "Can we see? The other boys probably don't know good art from a ten-pound gold nugget, but me—I'm right fond of . . . uh . . . *nature* scenes . . ."

Salvitch, who'd been a federal lawman at one time and who Longarm often partnered up with during poker matches at the Colorado Queen Saloon in Denver, glanced again at Longarm.

Longarm's ears warmed. Salvitch had seen it all and knew the score, and he was going to have some fun. Longarm doubted the man would spill the whole can of beans, but he'd let a few pintos dribble out for a laugh or two at his buddy's discomfort.

"Since when?" Longarm grunted, firing his nickel cheroot to cover his embarrassment.

"Yes, what is the subject of your painting, my dear?" chortled Miss May from the carriage, blinking against the still-sifting dust. "May we take a look?"

"Oh . . . I don't think so," Cynthia said, her normally red lips turning white. "The paint's not dry and . . . it loses its effect when . . . when the paint's not dry. Besides, I'm afraid it didn't turn out quite the way I expected, and I might just have to throw the whole thing away!"

"Balderdash!" intoned the general, rubbing the dust around on his spectacles with a silk hanky. "You're always your severest critic, Cynthia. Don't do anything hasty. When your aunt and I return from Leadville tomorrow, we'll have a look and help you judge with a pair of objective eyes."

Cynthia crossed her arms to support her unsupported breasts and said with a tad too much eagerness, "Leadville?"

"Yes, that's where we're headed. We've been invited by Baby Doe Tabor to join her and Mr. Tabor at the opera this evening. We'll be spending the night and returning in the morning. We should be home . . . oh, no later than noon tomorrow."

"You'll watch our girl for us this evening, won't you, Marshal Long?" the general inquired.

Longarm choked on a puff of cigar smoke and glanced at Reed Salvitch, who sat his bay gelding off the carriage's right rear wheel, grinning at him. "Of course, General. Don't worry about Miss Cynthia. When we're done out here with her painting and such, I'll see she makes it back to Grand View all right." He knew he was talking too much, making an ass out of himself, but his nerves were shot. "Fit as a fiddle—that's how you'll find your lovely niece tomorrow. 'Round noon, did you say?"

"Yes, around noon." Miss May arched a brow at Cynthia. "You'd best be getting back to town, dear. The sun is rather penetrating at these altitudes, and you wouldn't want to take too much color. Besides, Mrs. McQueen will be starting to worry . . ."

Mrs. Larimer regarded Longarm with a brow skeptically arched. Mrs. McQueen was the matronly old nurse whom the Larimers usually traveled with and who also acted as chaperone to the unwed young Larimer ladies. "She might begin to think that you and the good deputy here—"

"My bodyguard, Aunt May," Cynthia interjected, hooking one arm through the lawman's and somehow looking safe and secure while not wearing a stitch of underclothing. "Custis here is holding the uncouth frontiersmen at bay, of course, preventing a possible kidnapping or worse."

"Uh . . . yes," Aunt May said, shuttling a suspicious glance between the two. "Be that as it may, people do talk, my dear, and I think it best if you return to the hotel at once and try to spend as much time *indoors* from now on as possible. Surely there's as much to paint in the Arkansas River House as there is out . . ."

The old woman wrinkled her brow at Longarm once more, almost as though the old bat could see in his eyes his rock-hard cock standing at full mast and firmly embedded in her well-blooded niece's silky snatch.

"As there is out *here* . . ." Aunt May concluded.

"Of course, Aunt May," Cynthia said, her charming smile in place. Longarm's gut tightened when he saw some grass hanging in a wave of her black hair, a few inches from her shoulder. "We were just heading back to town now, as a matter of fact."

"I do appreciate your service, Marshal Long," the general chimed in, pinching the broad brim of his plumed cavalry hat at Longarm. "When it comes to my lovely niece, you go above and beyond the call of duty, dear sir. And for that, I am indeed grateful."

"Ah, heck," Longarm grunted, wondering if his cheeks were as red as they felt. Judging by the grins not only on Salvitch's face but on the faces of the other two Larimer bodyguards, they were. "Just glad I can be of help, General. Wouldn't want your niece to feel constrained in her Western travels, nor in any peril."

"Indeed, good sir!" the general said. "Well, Miss May, shall we?"

Miss May was scrutinizing Longarm again suspiciously, her thin gray brows beetled beneath the brim of her gaudy picture hat. "Yes, I suppose we'd best run along. Baby Doe will be wondering . . ."

Cynthia and her Western benefactors said good-bye, waving and blowing kisses, and the general and Mrs. Larimer rattled off in their carriage. All three bodyguards favored Longarm and the girl with a pinch of their hat brims, Salvitch giving his poker buddy a "you old dog" wink.

Then Longarm and the most beautiful girl on Colorado's western slope stood, hand in hand, watching the party fade over the next rise, the blue mountain upon which Leadville perched looming ahead of them.

Longarm rolled his smoldering cigar from one side of

his mouth to the other. "I haven't been that nervous since last Christmas, when the general damn near caught you giving me a blow job in his very own office."

Cynthia giggled.

"Speaking of which," she said, deftly lifting her skirt above her head and once more standing naked before him, "and seein' as how we're all alone once more . . . what do you say we have a little more fun before we head back to boring old town and I have to spend the remainder of the trip with boring old Mrs. McQueen?"

"Jesus," he groaned, chomping down on his cigar as the girl started unbuckling his cartridge belt. "You're gonna be the death of me yet—you know that?"

With a devilish snort, Cynthia knelt, opened his pants, fished his dong out of his underwear, and went to work.

Chapter 3

Grand View huddled in a broad canyon surrounded by brooding Gothic castles of towering granite that were fringed or streaked with dirty snow patches throughout the windy, high-altitude summer.

Skirted by the Arkansas River, flowing fast and frigid in its deep, wide gash sheathed in crenellated sandstone, the town was old—founded by Mexican goat herders and sheepherders over a century ago. It had been reinvigorated and reinvented within the past twenty years when prospectors and moneyed American mining outfits had discovered gold in most of the creeks and streams washing down the western canyons of the Continental Divide.

Now the town was fringed with tent shacks and wagon huts and Long Toms of sluice boxes snaking into the plethora of creeks bisecting the canyon. It also boasted a China-town of washhouses, hog pens, opium dens, and "dance" houses so loud and bawdy that they'd caught the attention of women's temperance societies as far away as Cincinnati.

But the town's brick-paved central business district boasted a theater, an opera house, luxury hotels, and eateries equaled only by those of cities ten times Grand View's size, and a hot springs frequented by the infirm, moneyed, and silver-spooned throughout the continent for its supposed healing properties.

A narrow-gauge railroad carried tourists over Evergreen Pass from Denver. That's how Longarm and the Larimers got here when Miss May, stove up by the "rheumatics" after a long Denver winter, decided it was time to loll in Grand View's hot spring baths for a week. Cynthia, being in Denver at the time after a winter in Italy, was naturally invited along.

The raven-haired heiress with more than a little flair for natural painting, among other talents, naturally invited her Denver "chaperone and platonic dinner companion" along for her protection and amusement. Since Longarm hadn't had a vacation in three years, and he couldn't resist the temptation of showing the sexy Larimer lass around the summery western slope, on her back and in every other position the two could come up with, he finagled a week of unpaid, well-deserved leave from his boss, Chief Marshal Billy Vail.

"Well, this'll be the end of ya," Billy had grumbled, tossing Longarm his approved leave papers.

"What's that, Chief?"

"When the general catches you and his niece doin' it doggy style and seven other ways from sundown along some creek up there at Grand View, he'll run you through with his saber. Skewer you—and deservedly so!—from one end to the other. And I'll be interviewing men to take your place by, oh"—Billy scratched his double chin in mock calculation as he studied his desk calendar—"I'd say the beginning of next week."

Longarm chuckled at the remembered conversation now

as he and Cynthia, having wined and dined along Aspen Creek and made their way astride a pair of rented horses down the long valley trail toward Grand View, entered the outskirts of the bustling burg.

"What do you find amusing, Custis?" Cynthia asked from beneath her broad-brimmed, bullet-crowned sombrero.

"I was just thinking about Billy Vail."

"You promised you wouldn't think about work out here!"

Longarm chuckled again. "It wasn't work I was thinking about. I was thinking how Billy's become as much of a soothsayer as an old crone I once met in the hills of eastern Kentucky."

"Oh?" Cynthia arched a quizzical brow. "How so?" She rode to his left along the dusty trail, her easel and the unmentionable canvas stowed in canvas pouches draped across her gelding's rump. Their picnic basket hung from Longarm's saddle horn.

"Oh . . ." The lawman hesitated, wishing suddenly he'd kept his trap shut.

Cynthia would have been horrified if she knew that Longarm's supervisor knew of their figurative and literal entanglements and had warned Longarm away from her.

"Oh, nothin'—just a couple wayward thoughts is all."

"Come on," Cynthia said encouragingly, smiling at him with gentle beseeching. "What did dear Mr. Vail foretell? He doesn't know . . . you know . . . about us, does he, Custis?"

Longarm was glad when an ore wagon from one of the local mines drew up behind them and they had to rein their horses off on opposite sides of the trail to let the mule skinners pass. He was just as glad when another wagon pulled away from the Grand View Bank and one of the two men in the driver's box shouted, "Custis Long, you old dog, *what the hell kinda mud you got yourself mired in now*? Ha! Ha! Ha!"

Longarm scowled up at the approaching wagon—an old Conestoga freighter with high sideboards and log chains attached to the double-tree for sharp cornering. The two men in the boot were both big and bearded. One carried a double-bore shotgun ready across his chest, while the other held the four-mule hitch's ribbons in his gloved hands.

He had a wooden leg with what looked like a railroad spike for a peg, and there was a lightninglike slash of knotted, pink flesh through his bushy, salt-and-pepper beard.

The familiar eyes were large and round and bright with humor and good cheer.

"Richard?" Longarm said, a frown wrinkling his chestnut brows. "Richard Collins—that you up there, you old mossyhorn?"

The bearded, one-legged man threw his head back on his shoulders, laughing heartily while pulling back on the mules' reins. As the wagon squawked to a halt in front of Longarm and Cynthia, the four outriders—all swarthy gents in dusty trail gear and holding Winchester rifles or shotguns across their saddle bows—drew to a halt as well.

"I'll be gawd-damned!" The one-legged man gained a horrified expression and doffed his battered leather hat, held it down over his chest, and regarded Cynthia with genuine chagrin. "I do beg your pardon, young lady. It's just that I thought this tall, handsome drink of water sittin' beside you was done dead and buried and chewed by coyotes near on a decade ago. But, 'less I'm seein' ghosts now since I parted ways with the jug an' fallen women, here he is in the flesh!"

Cynthia laughed with genuine mirth at the old-timer.

Longarm shook his head. "They haven't found the bullet that could stop me, Richard. Not that they haven't tried." He smiled and cuffed his hat back off his forehead. "How in the hell you been, Richard? To tell you the truth, I was starting to think *you* were dead. What's it been—ten, twelve years?"

"The last time I saw you, you'd just given up your evil ways to don a deputy U.S. marshal's badge." The driver glanced at Cynthia once more, his liquid-brown eyes fairly snapping with appreciation as they feasted on the girl's delightful form. "What'd you do—go and get a dose of the smarts and settle down with this pretty young lass here in Grand View?"

"I haven't gotten that smart . . ."

"Yet," Cynthia finished for him with her winning smile.

"Cynthia Larimer," Longarm said, "this old rapscallion is an old friend of mine—one of the first who'd tolerate me when I first crossed the Mississippi longer ago than I want to remember. Richard Collins, meet Cynthia Larimer."

"Holy shit on the parson's porch!" Collins said, eyes popping wide at Cynthia. "You mean to tell me you're of them high-rollin' Larimers from Denver—the ones that founded the whole damn town? And there I go again, so damn excited I keep using farm talk in the presence of a lady, and a high-bred one at that.

"I'm just embarrassin' myself all over the place! But I am sincerely pleased to make your acquaintance, Miss Larimer, and I hope you don't think ill of me. It ain't every day I get to meet a lady, let alone one as young and purty as you, and one—"

"All right, all right, enough of that," Longarm interrupted. "You're too old and gimpy for her, Richard. And

while she ain't been spoken for by me or anyone else . . .
yet . . . you'd have even less of a chance getting past the
general than I would!"

Longarm chuckled as he put his horse up beside the
driver's box and extended his hand to his old friend. "How
you been, you larcenous old diamondback?"

Collins chuckled as he shook Longarm's hand. "Fit as a
fiddle and then some." He stomped his peg leg on the floor
of the wagon box. "Still just as gimpy as that Comanche
arrow left me, and"—he glanced at Cynthia while he rubbed
the ugly scar on his bearded cheek—"just as ugly as the
horn of that riled bull buff left me back in '62, but I'm gettin' along just fine. Mule skinnin' for the mine company up
to Creed, don't ya know."

"The Silverjack Company?"

A couple of horseback riders and a long mule team
angled around him and the Conestoga sitting in the middle
of Grand View's main drag. No one seemed to mind the
inconvenience, he noticed, as all male eyes lingered without exception over Cynthia sitting her gelding's saddle
straight-backed and beautifully, smiling at Longarm's
long-lost friend while her raven hair jostled around in the
wind.

"Silverjack—that's the one." Collins hooked a thumb
toward the covered box behind him. "Me and the boys just
picked up the month's payroll and are fixin' to haul her up
to the mine office in Creed for payday on Friday. Helluva
nice-payin' job—a lot better'n hide skinnin' an' dodgin'
Comanch' arrows, I'll assure you of that, my young
friend!"

"Richard and I hunted buffalo together," Longarm told
Cynthia. "Longer ago than I care to remember." Returning

his glance to Collins, he said, "I sure wish we could sit down over a whiskey and beer or two, play a game of cards, and catch up."

"Nothin' would please me more, Custis," Collins said sincerely. "Maybe next time you're in the country. Like I said, I got this payroll to haul. And, dadblast it, a timetable to keep."

"How's Sue?" Longarm asked as he backed his bay away from the Conestoga.

Collins made a sad face and shook his head, his eyes instantly glazing, his voice thickening. "Dang heart trouble got her two years ago, Custis. Be two years and three months tomorrow. Can you believe I gotta go on without that gal? It troubles me dear, and you know, there ain't one dang thing I can do about it!"

Longarm shook his head and scowled. "I truly am sorry, Richard. To say Sue was a good woman is like sayin' the winter has some bite at this altitude."

"Nothin' you can say." Collins loosened the ribbons in his hands. "But now that I know you're still residin' on the green side of the sod, I'll look ya up sometime. I reckon you're still in Denver."

"In the Federal Building!" Longarm yelled as Collins slapped the ribbons over the mules' backs and the team lunged forward, braying and clomping and turning the finely ground dust.

Collins threw a hand up in acknowledgment, and then the wagon and the outriders headed on out of Grand View, the adobe-colored dust churning behind them.

"What a sad man," Cynthia said forlornly as she put her gelding up beside Longarm, who sat staring after his friend.

"Losing a woman like Sue would make anyone sad. I'll

have to hunt Richard down one of these days. He taught me
the ropes out here, and I saw him and Sue married in Tas-
cosa . . ."

"Longer ago than you wanna remember?"

Longarm glanced at Cynthia. She looked at him with a
bittersweet understanding that belied her young age. He'd
better be careful, he told himself, resisting the urge to kiss
her. A girl like Miss Cynthia Larimer could get under a
man's skin right deep. And besides the occasional frolic
when she was in the neighborhood, they had no future.

"Come on," he said. "Let's go somewhere respectable
and I'll buy you a lemonade."

"I don't want a lemonade. I want a brandy. Straight up.
With some good, dark chocolate truffles."

It wasn't too much later, sitting in the well-appointed
dining room of the Savage House, surrounded by the well-
attired, moneyed visitors of the local hot springs, that Longarm chuckled with Cynthia over their near-fatal escapade
up in the hills.

They'd been sitting there for a half hour when Longarm
glanced out the window and dropped his fork back down on
his dessert plate. The sharp ring of the silver on the fine
china caused a hush to befall the room.

"What is it?" Cynthia asked.

Longarm slid the lace curtains away from the window
beside him and stared into the main street of Grand View.
A frown gathered on his forehead and brow like a fast-
approaching thunderhead.

"Custis, what is it?" Cynthia asked again with concern,
placing her hand on his wrist.

"I think it's . . . *Richard*!" he grunted, rising so abruptly
that the table bounced, rattling dishes, silver, and brandy
goblets.

The other afternoon diners and two elegantly garbed waiters turned to him in shock and horror as he tossed his cloth napkin away and sprinted for the door, leaving Cynthia gaping behind him.

Chapter 4

A woman screamed as Longarm ran down the Savage House's broad wooden steps.

He glanced left along the street to see the horseback figure he'd seen from the window slump down his mount's right side and tumble onto the cobblestones paving the central business district.

Longarm ran toward the man, his string tie whipping out behind his neck. *"Richard!"*

People on both sides of Grand View's busy main drag stopped to regard the fallen figure. A couple of shop merchants stepped off their boardwalks to approach the man warily. Longarm pushed between two of these and dropped to a knee beside his old friend, who lay facedown on the cobblestones. The man's horse—one of the outriders' mounts apparently—edged away in fright. Longarm noticed it wore a long bullet crease across its right hip, and one ear was freshly notched.

Collins clutched both hands to his belly and kicked his high-topped, lace-up boots in agony, groaning.

Longarm set a hand on the man's shoulder. "Richard, what happened?"

"Ah, Custis . . ."

"What happened?"

"They . . . they hit the wagon. Was waitin' out by Dobie Springs . . . in them rocks . . ."

"Who did? How many?" Longarm paused to glance up at the shopkeepers crouching over him. "One of you stop gawkin' and fetch a sawbones pronto!"

A man with thick red muttonchops wheeled and shambled away.

Richard Collins lifted his head from the cobbled street. Frothy red blood spilled down his lower lip as he regarded Longarm with pain-pinched brown eyes. "There was seven of 'em," he said weakly. "One wore a long, green neckerchief like it was a flag or some damn thing."

A man's shout rose from behind Longarm: "What's going on there?"

Longarm glanced over his shoulder to see two men in wool suits and brown bowler hats and wearing copper deputy sheriff's stars on their lapels run toward him at an angle from up the street. They both wore sidearms, and one carried a sawed-off, double-barreled shotgun.

"A pill roller's on the way," Longarm said, easing Collins onto his back.

He winced when he saw the blood gushing from the man's belly and from another bullet hole higher up, over his left lung. As though reading the lawman's thoughts as he slumped against Longarm's thigh, Collins rolled his red-rimmed, pain-wracked eyes up to his younger friend and gave a wry smile.

"I'm glad I got to see ya one last time, Custis. Sorry we didn't have that drink . . ."

"Hold on, Richard."

"Step aside, step aside," ordered one of the sheriff's deputies approaching from behind.

Collins swallowed, winced, and said just barely loudly enough to be heard above the din of the growing crowd around him and Longarm, "They was headed south."

As Collins's eyes began to close, Longarm jerked the man's shoulders and rasped savagely, "I'll see they're caught, Richard! I promise—your hear me?"

"What's going on? Who is this man?"

Longarm glanced up at the tall deputy standing over him—a young man who took himself very seriously with his tailored suit, trimmed beard, and hooded brows, clutching a sawed-off Greener in both hands across the gold watch chain hanging from a pocket of his faun vest.

"Richard Collins," Longarm said, hearing the thickness in his voice as his old friend became a heavy, lifeless weight against his thigh. He gritted his teeth with fury. "He drove the payroll wagon for the Silverjack outfit. They got hit up the road, at a place called Dobie Springs. Get some men together and hightail it!"

"Dobie Springs?" the man with the shotgun said. Not waiting for a reply, he turned, pushed through the gathering crowd, and jogged up the street toward the sheriff's office two blocks away.

"They shot Ole Peg Leg?" the other deputy said—a redhead with a pale, freckled face and goatee and cobalt eyes. He stared with faint distaste at the wounded man slumped in the street before him.

Collins's gloved hands had fallen to his sides, and his eyes had closed. His chest was still.

Longarm felt a cold, tight knot in the back of his throat as he eased the man down onto the cobbles. Rising slowly, he turned to the redheaded deputy standing with his thumbs hooked behind his cartridge belt and chewing a matchstick with a slightly insolent air.

Rage bursting a dam inside him, Longarm suddenly grabbed the deputy by his coat lapels and jerked him straight up and pushed him backward.

The man gave a cry of shock and indignation as Longarm continued thrusting him up the street and growling, "What the hell are you doing standing here with your thumb up your yellow ass, you little pipsqueak? Saddle a horse and ride, you son of a *bitch*!"

"Hey!" the deputy exclaimed, tight-jawed and nearly falling over his own boots as Longarm released him suddenly.

The redhead closed his hand over the grips of the walnut-gripped .45 slung low on his right hip. As he started to bring it up, Longarm kicked the gun out of his hand and snarled, "I'm Custis Long, deputy United States marshal. I'm gonna take that horse over there," he said, pointing at Collins's mount standing in some shade on the opposite side of the street, "and head out to Dobie Springs. Keep that gun holstered once you pick it up, and tell Sheriff Dieter what I just told you. Can you handle that?"

Standing slump-shouldered, mouth agape, his gun hand angling out toward the Peacemaker that had fallen next to several large plops of horse dung, the man just stared at Longarm in shock.

"Move, goddamnit!" Longarm roared.

The redhead jerked to life. As he glanced at the crowd around Longarm, his face turned as red as his hair. He scooped up his revolver, brushed it off with an enraged air, and casting anther haughty glance at the federal lawman, holstered the piece and stalked up the street toward the sheriff's office.

Longarm looked toward the Savage House, where most of the diners now stood on the broad front porch staring over the timbered railing toward the crowd clustered around the dead man. Several held coffee cups; one leonine-headed gent in a burgundy frock smoked a cigar.

Longarm raked his frustrated gaze across the faces standing there, and called, *"Cynthia?"*

"Here."

Longarm whipped around. She knelt beside Richard Collins, within the ragged circle of standing onlookers. Her dress was speckled with blood, and one of her hands was soaked with it. Staring up at Longarm, her cheeks flushed with emotion, eyes glazed with tears, she said, "I heard, Custis. Go!"

Longarm wheeled and ran to the horse, which shied away at first. But he cornered it against the side of a fudge shop, grabbed the reins, and swung up into the saddle. Glancing back at the crowd in which Cynthia remained kneeling beside Richard, he spat angrily and batted his spurless heels against the buckskin's ribs.

The horse whinnied and lunged forward, clomping into an instant gallop down the street, weaving around horseback riders and wagons.

In less than a minute, he and the buckskin left the last of the adobe brick cabins and dilapidated corrals on the outskirts of the old town, and headed straight south through the sage and the boulders that had fallen from the many escarpments along both sides of the trail.

The trace meandered through wolf willows, cottonwoods, and sycamores lining the bank of the broiling Arkansas River. The recent furrows made by Richard's wagon were nearly pristine in the chalky dust. A bitter stone cemented itself in Longarm's chest as he followed the twin gashes, knowing that they were made less than an hour ago, when Richard was still alive. Now his old hide-hunting pal lay dead on the horse-soiled cobbles near the Savage House in Grand View.

Longarm felt as though he'd been badly cheated at a gambling table. He'd just seen his old friend for a few precious minutes after so many years. Now Richard was dead, and Longarm would never know how the old mossyhorn had spent the last dozen or so years.

Never throw back a few drinks with him in honor of his beloved Sue, a half-breed Ute from the White River country north of here.

Longarm didn't know the country well enough to know Dobie Springs, but it turned out he didn't need to know it to find the place. He knew it when he saw it, just a depression in a rocky, cottonwood-stippled hollow where someone— probably the local stage company—had built a large stone tank around the springs and piped the water out to hollowed pine logs for horse troughs.

The place was only a couple miles from town, but the team from the Silverjack had stopped here to fill their canteens, and likely the barrel attached to the side of the wagon. Apparently, they'd just started to fill up when they'd been hit by bushwhackers probably hunched and waiting in the clumps of brush and rocks around the spring.

Longarm dismounted and walked amidst the four outriders lying in twisted heaps before the stone tank. To a man, they'd been shot in the back. Some had taken several bullets. Only one appeared to have gotten his rifle cocked.

It lay between his spread legs, the hammer back, the cocking mechanism angled down from the trigger.

No spent cartridge casings were anywhere around the dead men.

Longarm walked up beside the wagon, which stood about ten feet from the spring, in the shade of a sprawling sycamore. The brake had been set, and the mules stood twitching their ears and glancing over their withers at Longarm, giving an occasional edgy bray. The canvas cover hung from a couple of the steel rings in the side of the box, dangling toward the ground to reveal the wagon's bed—empty except for the cut ropes that had secured the strongbox.

Longarm looked into the driver's boot. Blood, already nearly dry in these high, arid climes, stained the seat and the splintered gray dashboard on the driver's side. The shotgun rider had made it off the wagon, maybe while Richard was fooling with the brake and the ribbons and his peg leg, and he lay slumped forward now over the side of the water tank, bent knees pressed against the mortared stones.

The man's head and arms were in the water, which bubbled up from the mossy stones at the far side. Blood filmed the clear liquid, streaking the surface like spilled oil.

Longarm reached into the water, grabbed the man's collar, and pulled his head out. He eased the man down to the ground and saw that the bullet that had plowed through the back of his head had nearly pulverized his face, causing both eyes to bulge hideously from their sockets.

"Back-shooting scum," Longarm growled as he folded the dead man's arms over his chest, rested his hands in his lap, and avoided another look at those horrific eyes.

Longarm glanced at the wagon once more. Richard might have played possum while the robbers had grabbed the strongbox out of the wagon's bed. That would have been like the old frontiersman, who had survived multiple attacks by Indians and wild animals in his sixty-plus years west of the Mississippi, having come out here originally from Alabama.

When the robbers had pulled out, probably strapping the strongbox onto a mule or distributing the loot amongst themselves for lighter hauling, Richard had heaved himself onto the buckskin's back, and bent-necked it for town.

"Tough old dog," Longarm said with a grimace, casting his gaze southward. "And you saw where they were headed, too, didn't you? Well, you didn't go through all that for nothin'. I'll guaran-damn-tee you . . ."

He let his voice trail off as the thud of several sets of shod hooves sounded, growing steadily louder. He glanced toward town to see a handful of riders, silhouetted against the lake-blue sky, lunging toward him beneath a yellow, churning dust cloud. Rifles bristled up from wool-clad thighs, and copper badges flashed and winked from coat lapels.

Longarm stood at the rear of the pillaged wagon, holding the buckskin's reins, as the five deputies led by Sheriff Ed Dieter pulled up before him, dust sifting and tack squawking. Longarm knew Dieter only by reputation, knew he'd been a mine engineer for a time, then a cattle rancher, before running for office in Grand View.

He was a willowy strap of rawhide, fifty or older, whose face wasn't so much tanned as bleached by wind and sun, the skin shrunken across sharp cheekbones. He wore a brown suit and a high-crowned cream Stetson, and two pistols

bristled on his hips. The barrel of a pearl-gripped Colt protruded three inches below its soft brown holster, positioned
for a cross-draw.

The redheaded deputy whom Longarm had roughed up
in Grand View sat off the sheriff's right flank, regarding the
federal lawman sourly.

Narrowing his eyes at Longarm, Dieter barked, "Price,
Atkins—dismount and scour the brush for the loot!"

"You won't find it in the brush, Sheriff," Longarm said.
"Richard said they'd headed south with it."

"He was wounded," Dieter said, his mouth tight, his
voice deep and raspy. "He likely couldn't see *all* of the killers' movements. They might have hid the strongbox in the
brush with the intent to circle back for it later, after a posse
had passed. Those strongboxes are heavy, and you need
time to get away with one. I'm not new to this job, mister.
And this ain't my first rodeo."

As two deputies scoured the shrubs and rocks around the
spring, the sheriff slitted his washed-out eyes even further
at Longarm. "Now, who the hell are you, and why are you
here?"

"Like I told Red here, I'm Custis Long, deputy U.S.
marshal out of Denver." Longarm opened his mouth to continue, but before he could bark out any more words, Dieter
snapped a gray-gloved hand up, cutting him off.

"Are you here on official government business?"

"No, I'm—"

"Then kindly butt out," Dieter ordered, setting his jaws
and blinking his catlike eyes. He canted his head toward the
redhead. "Kennedy here told me you accosted him on the
street in front of Grand View citizens. You had no business
doing that, as you have no jurisdiction here. If I didn't have

a passel of outlaws to chase, I'd have you in irons and haul your federal ass back to jail, let Billy Vail in Denver come bail you out!"

Dieter was mad, but Longarm was madder. Taking one step toward the sheriff, whipping the bucksin's reins in frustration, and bending forward at the waist, he rasped, "Those men killed a friend of mine, Dieter, and I don't intend to let them get away. I may not have started out here in an official capacity, but I sure as hell—!"

"You'll return to Grand View and stay out of county business!" Dieter roared, rising up in his saddle. "If you insist on interfering, I'll have one of my deputies arrest you and drag you back to the Arkansas County lockup. If you think I won't, just push me, Long! My men and I are trained professionals. We'll run these killers down and we'll secure the strongbox—by sundown if not sooner."

Spit flecked Dieter's lower white lip as his voice rose so shrilly it cracked. "But only if you'll get the holy fuck out of our way so we can!"

Longarm relaxed his shoulders with defeat. The man had him beat. Longarm had no authority here; he was under the jurisdiction of Sheriff Dieter. He had no doubt the man would carry through with his threat of arresting him if he tried to "interfere." Or he'd *try* to arrest him, and there'd be hell to pay on both sides.

Longarm only wanted to help get the men who'd murdered his friend, but these local lawmen were touchy about federal assistance. He'd best step aside, let them do their work. If they could.

He'd be damned if he wouldn't hang around and make sure they could.

The men who'd attacked the payroll shipment were

seasoned, cold-blooded killers. Longarm wasn't sure Dieter and his four deputies were up to the task of bringing them down. He would have suggested they organize a posse, but posses take time to organize. The killers could be holed up deep in one of the many mountain ranges around here by the time the sheriff pulled a group together.

"Anything?" Dieter called to the men stomping around in the shrubs around the spring.

"Nothin', Sheriff," called the one named Price, who, decked out in a nicely cut black suit and with a blond spade beard, looked little older than twenty-two or twenty-three.

"Then get the hell back here and mount your horses," Dieter said, still eyeing Longarm angrily.

As Price and Atkins strode back to their horses, the reins of which were being held by one of the other mounted deputies, Dieter reached inside the pocket of his tan vest and flipped a coin in the air toward Longarm.

"Here you go, mister," the sheriff said with a sneer. "Go on back to Grand View and cool your heels on me."

Longarm automatically raked the coin out of the air and opened his palm to see the silver dollar winking up at him.

He glowered back at Dieter, but held his tongue while the sheriff reined around him and booted his steeldust gelding south along the curving, two-track trail through the sage. Kennedy wrinkled his nose and gritted his teeth at Longarm as he put his line-back dun after the sheriff. The other four badge toters followed suit, two of the men turning their heads to give Longarm mocking glances before looking at each other and chuckling caustically as they booted their mounts into dust-churning gallops.

In minutes, the lawmen were gone, their hoof thuds

dwindling, dust sifting behind them around Longarm, who stared after them, hard-eyed.

"Well, hell, fellas," he grumbled, flipping the silver dollar in the air, then dropping it into his vest pocket. "Good goddamn luck."

Chapter 5

Longarm rode back to Grand View feeling testy as a caged cat.

But now that his blood had cooled, he realized that even if Dieter had wanted his help in running the killers to ground, he'd be of little use on the worn-out, bullet-grazed buckskin and with only his Colt for weaponry. He'd left his Winchester '73 in his hotel room, and while he was handy with the double-action pistol, he felt a whole lot more comfortable confronting professional long riders with a fresh horse and a repeating rifle.

When he rode into town, he found business as usual on the main drag . . . except for Richard Collins's blood staining the cobbles just down the street from the Savage House. He learned from the constable whom Dieter had left in charge that Richard had been taken to one of the three local undertakers. After Longarm had tracked down and given the bone planter, a smarmy but seemingly trustworthy gent named Zachariah T. Rose, enough money to make sure Richard would be planted attired in a new black suit and the best wooden overcoat to be found in Rose's shed, and after a few words from the Good Book were read over him, the federal lawman headed to one of the little Mexican cantinas near the river for a couple shots of tequila on Dieter's dollar.

He'd considered letting Cynthia know he was back, but decided against it. In a foul mood, he wanted time to himself where he felt the most comfortable—drinking rotgut tequila and warm beer in a smoky, shadowy tavern on the wrong side of the tracks, with goats bleating and chickens clucking outside the beaded-door curtain, and maybe nibbling carne asada and warm corn tortillas when the liquor burned a hole in his gut.

A couple of young *putas* came up to him, rubbing their breasts against his shoulder. One lifted his hand up her flour-sack smock, caressing the small, round orb with his palm, intoning, "You don like? You don like?"

Sated by his tumbles with Cynthia earlier, he waved them away and called for another beer and another tequila shot, and scratched the ears of the old cur dreaming beneath his bench.

Frustration burned in him.

He'd often thought about Richard Collins, the way you do about old friends you hadn't seen in a while, wondering how and where they were, if they were still alive. But you get too busy and caught up in your job and daily routine to let it go any further than wondering until it's too late.

And then you wonder why you only wondered, because they're gone and they won't be back.

For Longarm, it was all the more confounding because he'd just seen the man and was ripe with the prospect of seeking him out again and learning more about his life, only to cradle his friend in his arms a half hour later and watch him die at the hands of cutthroats headed south with a strongbox of stolen loot.

When he'd eaten, he listened to the three-piece band for a while, but neither the food nor drink nor music picked his spirits up, so he mashed his hat down on his head, raked his Winchester off the table, and tramped back to the right side of the tracks.

He checked at the sheriff's office. The constable, a portly, middle-aged gent who was reading an illustrated newspaper at the sheriff's tidy desk, yawned and told Long-arm he'd seen nothing of the posse yet.

Longarm wasn't surprised. He resisted the urge to rent a mount at the livery stable and set out after them. It was good dark and there was no moon and he'd only waste time stumbling around out in the Colorado mountains and can-yons in the dark, which, in spite of the sparkling stars, was like the inside of a black leather glove.

He decided to wait and see what tomorrow would bring. If the posse wasn't back by noon, he'd rent that horse and fog the trail south. Leaving the sheriff's finely appointed office and the constable yawning, sipping black coffee, and turning pulp pages, he headed back to his hotel on a side street behind the Savage House.

His digs in the Headwaters Inn were considerably more modest than the Larimers', and even if he'd had the money or allowed the general to pay his way, he wouldn't have trusted himself or Cynthia in the same building together. Tonight, he wouldn't have slept any better in one of the Savage House's fine feather beds anyway. He tossed and turned all night with convoluted dreams involving gunfire, screams, and buffalo stampedes.

There was even a howling Comanche in one segment, just after he'd gone back to bed after evacuating his bladder in the thunder mug, and then a pistol shot loud enough to have been fired a foot away jerked his head up from his pillow at dawn.

After a whore's bath and a breakfast of eggs, potatoes, sausage, and hot black coffee in a café housed in the side shed off the Headwaters, he headed toward Main Street. He was almost there, walking up a deserted side street, when he stopped suddenly.

A horse clomped along the cobbles of the main drag, heading from left to right in front of Longarm. The horse was saddled, and its empty stirrups flapped against its ribs. Its reins trailed behind, broken and frayed from being stepped on. It was a big, rangy, line-back dun with a crooked white line down its snout.

As the horse passed behind the building on Longarm's right, its shod hooves echoing off the cobbles, the lawman's pulse quickened. He lengthened his stride and turned the corner onto the main drag. The horse continued heading away from him, down the middle of the street, its light brown tail hanging straight down between its legs.

A shop owner stopped sweeping the boardwalk in front of his drugstore to regard the horse curiously, then, frowning behind his wire spectacles, continued swiping at the scuffed manure dried into his boardwalk.

Longarm bent his legs in the direction of the fleeing horse, passing the druggist and continuing up the street until, rounding a bend, he saw the horse standing with four others in front of Lew Patten's Livery and Feed Barn. Patten had his front doors open, and the liveryman himself—a curly bearded, corpulent gent in a checked shirt beneath a canvas vest—stood inspecting the new horse as though it had dropped out of the sky.

Longarm knew the man from having rented his and Cynthia's mounts from him the previous day.

"Lew," he said, frowning as he approached, raking his gaze across the four saddled, riderless horses. "Aren't these . . . ?"

"They sure as shit are," Patten said, scowling over the line-back's neck. "These are the mounts I sent the lawdogs out on earlier." He jerked his head and walked down to the line-back's hindquarters. "Look here."

Longarm met the liveryman at the horse's tail, and he followed the man's grimy, sausage-sized finger as it traced a bullet burn across the mount's left hip.

"And here," Patten said, moving his hand up to a heavy blood smear stretching from the saddle's cantle across the slicker-wrapped bedroll to fade off into the top of the horse's tail.

Longarm ran his hand through the smear, then rubbed his fingers together. "Dry. These saddles were emptied sometime last night."

He turned to the liveryman, who stared at him horrified, mouth open. "Saddle me a good one, Lew. A stout one, with plenty of bottom. Make that two . . . and grain 'em good. I'll be back soon as I fetch my saddlebags and war sack."

Longarm's return to the liveryman wasn't quite that fast. When he'd retrieved his possibles from his room at the Headwaters and turned in his key, he tramped over to the Savage House and scratched out a note on hotel stationery while the morning desk clerk stood yawning with his be-ringed hands resting on the varnished mahogany counter.

Dear Cynthia,

Sorry I won't be making the return train trip with you to Denver. Sheriff's and deputies' mounts came back with empty saddles. With luck, I'll be back to Denver before you light out again for wherever.

With my apologies and affection,
your obedient servant,
Custis.

He shoved the note into a small, ivory envelope, licked it closed, scrawled Cynthia's name on it, and handed it over to the desk clerk. Distracted, he didn't realize that the man's expectant look meant that he was waiting for a tip, until Longarm was halfway to the train station to write out a telegraph message to Billy Vail.

He bit his cheek as he penciled the terse note, knowing Billy would be smoking mad when he found out Longarm had gone after a gang of cutthroats without assistance, especially after they'd killed five local lawmen and even though it wasn't officially any of Longarm's affair.

But he figured he'd better let his boss know what he was up to since it was doubtful he'd make it back to work next Monday, only two days away.

He paid the telegrapher and walked away from the plank-board shack abutting the narrow-gauge railroad tracks, hearing the key clacking away behind him, and strode over to the livery barn. Lew Patten had two horses waiting for him in the street where the lawmen's five mounts had been standing a half hour ago—one saddled, the other wearing a hackamore to which a ten-foot lead rope was hooked. They were both big, rangy horses—a pinto and a blue roan that looked like they could handle both mountain and plain at a ground-eating clip if needed.

The constable was there as well, looking nervous as he repeatedly lifted his derby hat to run his hands through his thin, sandy hair. "Christalmighty," the man said as Longarm strapped his rifle boot to his saddle. "Five missing badge toters . . . and, jumpin' Jehovah, I ain't no lawman! I just keep an eye on things when the sheriff and his men are outta town. Hell, I don't even know the law!"

"You know right from wrong, don't ya?" Longarm grunted, buckling the boot strap.

"Well . . . sure, but—"

"Then you can hold things down for a few days till I get back. If worse comes to worst and the sheriff is dead, you best have your town council call an emergency meeting and see about holding an election to get a new lawman seated pronto."

"He might just be wounded and layin' under a shrub out there," Patten hopefully opined as he held the bridle of the saddled pinto. "Same with his deputies. I can't see that gang takin' all *five* of 'em down. They ain't no tinhorns. They're good lawmen!"

"We'll see." Longarm hooked his war bag and canteen over his saddle horn, then took the reins from Patten and stepped into the leather. He nodded at both men, who were looking up at him with lost, confused expressions. "If my luck holds, I'll be back soon."

"And if it don't?" the constable asked.

Longarm swung the pinto around and, jerking the roan along behind him, booted the mount south along the cobbled main drag. "Then I won't be back at all."

Chapter 6

A little after noon, buzzards led Longarm to a broad cottonwood tree on the bank of a dry arroyo.

As his horse rounded a bend in the wash, following the cacophony kicked up by the frenzied birds, he sucked air through his teeth and jerked back on the pinto's reins, one hand closing automatically over the grips of his cross-draw .44.

The four deputies hung from a stout branch over the arroyo, the snow-spotted peaks of the Sawatch showing through the leaves and branches behind them. The lawmen's hands had been tied behind their backs. Three of the men had been shot, dried blood staining their twenty-dollar suits. Their holsters were empty, and the toes of their dusty boots angled toward the ground three feet below.

The hang ropes turned this way and that on the breeze and from the weight of the large, bald-headed turkey buzzards fluttering around the carrion, plucking flesh from their cheeks and necks and eye sockets. One bird glared at Longarm with its beady, oily black eyes, then, perched on Deputy Kennedy's shoulder, jerked its horrific head and bloody beak around to take a bite out of the deputy's swollen tongue protruding from between cracked, swollen lips.

The deputy seemed to glare spitefully down at Longarm, while the others stared forlornly into the brush around their stiffly turning bodies.

Feeling sick and muttering angry curses under his breath—the fools had obviously ridden into an ambush—Longarm scoured the brush around the four hanging corpses, but saw no sign of Dieter.

Could the sheriff have been taken hostage? Or had the man slipped away to hole up farther down the wash, dying slowly from his wounds?

Longarm cut the deputies down, but having no shovel with which to bury them, laid them out side by side in the shade. There was nothing he could do about the buzzards, so he just left the dead men there, shaking his head in frustration. He'd send an undertaker from Grand View to retrieve what was left of them later. Stepping back into the pinto's saddle, he continued trailing the fresh tracks he'd been following from Dobie Springs.

He galloped, pushing the horses hard, for another twenty minutes. Rounding a long bend in the stage road marked with four sets of relatively fresh horse tracks and occasional apple piles, he again jerked back on the pinto's reins.

A deep frown mantled his cinnamon brows and, slowly, as he booted the pinto ahead at an edgy, snorting trot, a look of revulsion cut deep into his rugged, sunburned features.

His brain was slow to believe the signals his eyes were firing into it. But as he and the horses drew closer to the object mounted on a gnarled cedar branch protruding from the trail's right side, he could no longer deny that the object was a man's head.

It was Sheriff Dieter's head minus its hat, its eyes droopy, the pale lips stretched back from its teeth in an eternal death snarl. Below the ragged folds of cut skin at the neck, the branch was coated with thick, dried blood.

Longarm's gut tightened as he stared down at the killers' grisly warning to anyone else thinking about fogging their trail, and all animosity for the sheriff dwindled. Dieter was obviously an arrogant fool who had overestimated his abilities, and had made some bad mistakes out here. Deadly mistakes. But no man deserved to be desecrated in this way.

A magpie swooped down from a cedar left of the trail. Screeching raucously, it landed on the sheriff's dusty, sweat-matted cap of thin, pewter hair and, aiming its pellet-sized, obsidian eyes at Longarm, gave another, proprietary scream. It lighted again and settled in a dead sycamore on the other side of the trail, where three other magpies were perched, acrimoniously staring down at the interloper.

From the pinto's back, Longarm—sick, cold, and furious—looked around for the rest of Dieter. Finally, with a confounded grunt, he swung down out of the leather and tied the horses, both fidgeting at the grisly sight and the death smell, to a tree several yards from the staked head.

He scoured the brush on both sides of the trail until he found the man's bloody corpse lying on its stomach at the bottom of a deep gully. Like the deputies', the sheriff's hands had been tied behind his back. Longarm didn't take a close look, as even from several feet away, the death stench burned his eyes and peppered his nose, but it was obvious Dieter had been shot several times.

Tortured, likely, as well.

By fork-tailed demons.

As with the others, Longarm didn't take time to bury the man. The sky was quickly purpling in the north, and distant thunder rumbled. He had to get back on the jackals' trail before the approaching rainstorm washed it out.

Returning to the trace, he pulled the stake out of the ground, carried the head over to the rest of Dieter, and using his boot to dislodge the head from the branch, dropped it into the gully on top of the man's body.

He kicked an overhanging lip of the gully onto both and, his lungs pinching and throat tightening at the sight of the carnage and the fetor of sun-seasoned rot, headed back to the horses. He switched his saddle from the pinto to the roan, watered both horses from his hat, and mounted up.

Nibbling the end off a nickel cheroot to help clear the cloying smell from his mouth and nose, he glanced toward the gully where the sheriff's corpse lay.

Longarm had run down his share of savage outlaws over the years—men so savage that if you likened them to animals, you'd insult grizzlies and wolves—but whoever had killed Dieter and the deputies were true, blue, yellow-toothed demons straight from the burning bowels of Hell. The urgent need to run them down before they could do the same to others, or even worse, tightened his shoulders and hardened his jaws.

"Gidup," he clucked to the roan, tugging on the lead rope.

He was too good a lawman to admit it, but he was glad he wasn't out here on official orders, for the men he was trailing deserved no official restraint. When he caught up to them, they were going to wish like hell he hadn't.

"Let's go." He glanced over his shoulder at the approaching purple, anvil-shaped storm just as another, louder thunderclap rumbled and echoed around the ridges. He leaned forward and, eyeing the clouds, patted the roan's withers. "Got some ground to cover, fellas."

"Halloo the camp!" he yelled later that night above the pounding rain and drumming thunder.

He'd seen the flicker of a campfire off the trail to his right and up a rocky slope amidst the wind-jostled shrubs and pines, and headed for it as the rain filled every ravine and hollow around him. He figured it was around ten o'clock, and it was as black as the bottom of a well between lightning flashes.

"Come in slow," a low voice growled beneath the storm.

Beneath the canopy of a couple of arching fir bows, Longarm swung down from the roan's saddle. He loosened each horse's latigo cinch, slipped their bits, then retrieved his tin coffee cup from a saddle pouch.

He left his Winchester in its boot and, trying hard to fashion a warm smile while lifting the flap of his rain slicker above his .44's handle, stepped over deadfall and around rocks toward the firelight reflected by a lean-to shelter flanked by a stony ridge.

Two men sat beneath the shelter, behind the leaping fire, steaming cups in their hands. Grimly, the unshaven men in yellow rain slickers like Longarm's watched the lawman approach the edge of the firelight, rain sluicing off his hat brim.

Longarm held up his coffee cup. "I'd be obliged for a cup of that coffee," he said loudly enough to be heard above the hammering storm, shivering as rain dribbled from an overhanging branch and down under his slicker, a chill finger tracing the line of his backbone.

The men stared at him, stony-faced. One was slender

with curly hair falling from beneath his funnel-brimmed Stetson. The other was a burly, bearded gent with a broad chest, heavy paunch, and thick legs angled out beside him. He rested one arm on an upraised knee. A rifle leaned nearby.

He flicked his hand up in a gesture of reluctant welcome.

Longarm continued forward, until the shelter hung over him, giving him some relief from the rain, and knelt before the fire. "Much obliged," he said, using a leather swatch to lift the pot from the fire and to tip it over his cup.

Aromatic steam wafted on the chill, damp air. Miles back, he'd discovered that the kill-crazy lobos he was hunting had separated into groups of twos and threes, scattering. But he wasn't too tired and frustrated to appreciate the smell of hot coffee on a stormy night.

He sat on a rock across the fire from the two men, who continued to regard him grimly. The flickering light showed their sunburned skin drawn taut across their cheekbones. They'd ridden far and hard. Longarm heard the snorts and stomps of their horses tied to a picket rope off to his right.

He rested his elbows on his knees and sipped the coffee.

"Tough night to be out," said the curly-haired gent. His gray blue eyes bored over the fire at Longarm.

"Wouldn't mind a warm feather bed!"

The big man ran his gaze across Longarm and curled his nose slightly. "Line rider?"

Longarm shrugged and purposely kept his good-natured smile in place. "I quit that ten years ago. Too damn many saddle galls!" Chuckling, he raised the cup to his lips and sipped.

The two men beneath the tarpaulin turned their heads, glancing at each other, incredulity showing in their rugged faces. Then they turned back to Longarm, eyes filled with the wariness of hunted animals.

Animals, all right. Longarm remembered Dieter's corpseless head staring at him from atop the stick beside the trail.

"Where you from?" asked the curly-haired man in the relative quiet after an earth-racking thunderclap.

"Grand View," Longarm said, taking another sip of the coffee. "You?"

The men stared at him in silence, but he could sense the blood warming and quickening in their veins.

"Leadville." The gent with the curly hair switched his coffee cup to his left hand, then slowly reached forward to shove a pine branch into the fire.

The fire snapped and popped. The coffeepot chugged.

Longarm lifted his cup to his lips with both hands. When he'd taken a sip, he turned the cup in his hands, switching it to his left, leaving the right one free. At the same time, he saw the big gent's eyes flick toward the Winchester rifle leaning against the log he was sitting on, two feet away from him.

"Heard there was a robbery up near Grand View," the curly-haired gent said conversationally, worrying his boot toe against a rock of the fire ring. "Bloody one. Quite a few men killed."

"More killed later." Longarm paused, raked his gaze between the two men whose hard eyes danced in the firelight. "Five lawmen. Came upon 'em just after noon. Savages cut the sheriff's head off, staked it along the trail."

"What some men won't do," said the curly-headed gent.

"Ain't that the truth?" Longarm said

The big man said nothing. He glowered across the fire at the newcomer, his right hand splayed across the thigh of his black denims.

The curly-headed gent used the leather swatch to pick up the coffeepot. "More belly wash?"

"Don't mind if I do."

Longarm thrust his cup forward. The curly-headed gent filled it, then splashed some into his own. He didn't offer any to the big man before returning the dented black pot to its flat rock beside the dancing flames.

Keeping his face implacable, he lifted his chin at Longarm. "What brings you down thisaway?"

"Those kill-crazy savages—that's what. Name's Long. Custis Long. Deputy U.S. marshal out of Denver."

"Kind outta your jurisdiction—ain't ya, Long?"

Longarm sipped his coffee and nodded. "One of the men they killed with the Silverjack wagon—the one-legged jehu—was a friend of mine." He ran his tongue across his front teeth, containing his rage. "A very good friend I hadn't seen in a while."

"That's a shame." The curly-haired gent lowered his chin slightly and rolled his eyes to regard the big man furtively. Sweat shone on his red brown forehead. "Reckon you won't get to see him at all again now."

Sucking a sharp breath, he worried his boot toe against the rock again and said, "So, these killers . . . you run any of 'em down yet?"

Longarm had just sipped his coffee. He held it in his mouth for a moment, then swallowed it with a faint gurgling sound as he stared up from beneath his mantled brows at the two men sitting across the fire. "Just you two."

A silence fell—one so heavy that it drowned out the the rain, the wind, the thunder, the snapping flames.

The two lobos stared across the fire at Longarm. Their eyes, shaded now by their brows, were as flat as pennies. They could have been two statues sitting there in the shadows shunted by the flickering, sparking flames.

It happened so fast that Longarm wasn't even sure which man he'd shot first before the flicker of movement across the fire caught his eye, and with an automatic movement driven more by instinct than thought, his double-action Colt was leaping and roaring in his hand.

He wasn't sure either how many times he'd fired the pistol until he heaved himself to his feet, the smell of cordite pungent beneath the tarpaulin, and flicked the loading gate open.

Stepping around the fire toward the two men lying in twisted heaps back against the base of the stony ridge, he pinched out four spent cartridge casings, heard them clatter onto the stones at his feet. Automatically, he plucked four fresh ones from his cartridge belt and thumbed them into the empty, smoking chambers of the cylinder.

Flicking the loading gate closed, he spun the cylinder and stared down at the curly-haired gent in grim satisfaction.

The man stared back at him, but his gray blue eyes were death-glazed. Yet they somehow retained the shock they'd acquired when the first bullet had punched through his heart, the second one following two inches to the right of the first.

Longarm stepped over the curly-haired gent and stared down at the big man. The big man stared back at him as well, but his thick lips moved slightly inside the heavy, gray brown beard. A spit bubble formed between them. He made a sound deep in his throat, just loud enough for Longarm to hear above the continuing rain.

Longarm dropped to a knee.

The man winced. Another spit bubble formed beside the first. Then the two bubbles popped at the same time. Blood pumped from his upper left chest and his belly.

"Son of a bitch," he raked out, the skin at the bridge of his broad nose wrinkling.

Longarm draped his gun hand across his knee and regarded the dying man coldly. "Where're the others headed? The same place? Or did they already divvy up the loot and scatter?"

The big man's nose curled as he hardened his jaws.

Longarm lowered his .44 to the man's belly, prodded the bloody hole with the barrel. The big man stiffened, and horror shone in his dung-brown eyes.

"I can either end your misery quick, or send you off howlin' like a stuck pig."

"Gnnahhh," the man said through a pained grimace, glaring up at Longarm.

The lawman pressed the Colt's barrel deeper into the hole.

The man's body tensed again, and the color leached out of his face. He whimpered, squirmed, and said something Longarm couldn't hear.

"What's that?"

The man lifted his fingers from the ground, curling them toward him.

Keeping the Colt pressed into the belly wound, Longarm lowered his head and turned his ear to the man's face.

The man breathed raggedly. He groaned, grunted, swallowed, and whispered, "Cimarron."

Longarm looked at him. "All of 'em headed there?"

The man blinked. Longarm took it for a nod.

He stood and angled his Colt at the man's forehead. "Say hi to Scratch for me, you murderin' dog."

The shot was drowned by a thunderclap.

Chapter 7

Longarm dragged the two dead men out away from their bivouac, dumped their carcasses in a rain-swollen gully, and watched them float away on the churning current—food for the mountain lions and wolves.

Returning to the camp, he unsaddled, fed, and watered his own horses, and tied them out with the others. After a simple but replenishing meal of jerky and some biscuits he found in the dead men's saddlebags, he had another cup of coffee, then rolled up in his soogan and listened to the mountain storm gradually drum itself out before he slept.

He woke at dawn and turned the dead men's horses loose. They'd likely be picked up by one of the sprawling ranches in this country, or they'd head back to where they'd come from. After a breakfast of coffee, jerky, and more of the dead men's biscuits, he saddled up, mounted, and headed in what he figured was the general direction of Cimarron.

He knew little about the town—only that it was a little gold and silver burg supplemented by ranchers who supplied beef to the mines in the Sangre de Cristos that loomed

southeast of it, and that it sprawled along a yucca and sage
flat along the Cimarron River. He'd been through there before, as the town lay just west of the Gunnison River along
one of the few routes to Colorado's western slope and the
Utah Territory.

Getting there from where he was now, somewhere north
and east of it, he figured—with the Sawatch and Granite
ranges as well as a rain-swollen river or two impeding his
way—would be tricky and time-consuming.

That, likely, was why the owlhoots had chosen it. Feeling skittish after their wanton killing of the five lawmen
from Grand View, they'd figure a posse would follow. The
route to Cimarron would give them plenty of time and op-
portunities to shed their pursuers. Or to simply confound
them and wear them out.

Scattering had been smart.

They were smart men. Or at least ramrodded by a smart
leader.

But they hadn't figured on the fat man giving away their
destination. And they hadn't figured on being trailed by a
man who didn't easily confound or wear out.

Or a man who was royally piss-burned that they'd killed
his old friend, Richard Collins.

Longarm would either beat them to Cimarron or arrive
nipping at their heels, and foil their probable plan of divvy-
ing up the Silverjack loot and parting ways for the last time,
each likely taking a different route to Old Mexico.

Longarm was riding the pinto when the horse snorted
and twitched its ears. He could feel the muscles beneath the
saddle bunch and tense.

"What is it, hoss?" Longarm muttered, looking around
at the rain-soggy sage and cedars humping around him, lit
by the mid-morning sun. "What now?"

Behind him, the roan nickered and bobbed its head.

Then Longarm saw what the horses had sensed—three long-haired riders traversing a hogback about two hundred yards away on his left flank. The riders wore no hats—only bandannas knotted around their foreheads. Their horses wore no saddles—only braided hemp or leather hackamores adorned with tribal feathers. On the horses' backs were only striped saddle blankets.

Longarm was too far away from the riders to see clearly, but he'd have bet gold dust to beans they were Indians—Utes or Southern Cheyenne. The knowledge sent a cricket of apprehension skittering along his spine.

Most of the Indians out here had been confined to reservations. But there weren't near enough cavalry to make sure they stayed there growing hay and raising cattle. Those that took umbrage to the system and jumped the rez usually had a hump in their necks for white folks, and stories of their depredations were common.

An hour after spying the three shadowing Indians, he halted his horses at the lip of the cut through which Bayonet Creek meandered. Only, in the wake of the storm, it wasn't so much meandering as churning up to nearly the lip of its chalky banks. As the water gurgled over hung-up drift logs and boulders, Longarm glanced over his shoulder.

It took him a minute to pick them out of the rolling, sage-stippled plateau—two silhouettes sitting their ponies near the lip of a low hogback while the third Indian stood beside his mount lower down the hill. He had his hands down around his crotch, and he was bending his knees slightly as he stared toward Longarm.

Pissing.

"Same to you," the lawman growled as he neck-reined the pinto on down the stream, looking for a place to cross that wouldn't sweep him into the Black Canyon of the Gunnison and to a watery grave farther west.

When he found a relatively wide, shallow ford, he took one more look behind him. The three Indians were cantering toward him across the sage flat, meandering around a couple of cabin-sized boulders left by the last glacier to rumble through this valley.

They weren't trying to overtake him. Not yet. They were just keeping pace, biding their time . . .

Longarm put the pinto into the creek, pulling the roan along behind. He sucked a sharp breath when the cold water inched up to his thighs, filling his boots.

The creek was deep enough so that the horses had to swim for about ten yards in the middle as they edged downstream. Then they regained their footing, splashed to the opposite shore, and lumbered up the steep, eroded bank.

Glancing back once more as both horses shook water from their backs, Longarm saw the three Indians approaching the place upstream where he'd stopped a few minutes ago. They weren't looking at him now, but down, judging the current below their foraging ponies.

Longarm reined his horses west and angled away from the creek and into the high hills known as the Antelope Buttes, the snow-spotted Sangre de Cristos rising, cool and blue, on his left, the Sawatch on his right. He hadn't ridden more than a couple of miles before he came to another deep cut in the floor of the plateau and stopped his horses, staring down the slope, lines of consternation carving into his sun-leathered forehead.

"For chrissakes," he grumbled, then booted the pinto on down the ridge, twisting around jutting sandstone scarps and cedars as he headed for the canvas-covered freight wagon firmly mired in a shallow stream that fed Bayonet Creek to the north.

The wagon had nearly made it across the flooded wash, but had hung up about twenty yards from the far side, its two mules bogged and frozen, standing in the muddy water and twitching their ears in typical mulish refusal. Two freighters were in the water, jerking on lead ropes tied to the pair's collars, while another popped a blacksnake over the stubborn animals' broad, mud-smeared backs and cursed loudly enough to be heard as far away as Missouri.

"Get along there, you mangy, yalla cayuses!" the driver bellowed, cracking the snake's popper once more over the leader's twitching ears. "Haul your filthy fuckin' asses on outta here or so help me I'll have ya both fer supper!"

Whip-crack!

"Hold on, you stupid son of a bitch!" Longarm bellowed as he splashed up beside the wagon and as the driver—a bearded bulldog in a red and black shirt and suspenders—began to swing the whip for another crack. "All you're doin' is scaring the bejesus out of those mules, and they're not gonna move if they're scared of both you *and* the mud!"

The whip sagged into the water in front of the wagon as the old man scowled at Longarm, one hand reaching for the Springfield carbine leaning against the driver's seat. "Who the fuck're you?"

"The man who's gonna end your misery right here and now if you keep reaching for that old army rifle."

The man stayed his hand and turned his head slightly, narrowing a deep-set eye as he regarded Longarm warily.

The lawman turned to the two freighters who'd stopped

jerking on the lead ropes. "Do you three dumb bastards make it a habit of . . . ?"

He let his voice trail off when he saw that one of the freighters was a pretty, freckle-faced blonde shading her eyes with one hand as she squinted up at Longarm from in front of the left mule . . . and that she wasn't wearing anything but a low-cut camisole and knee-length pantaloons.

Both garments were wet and mud-splattered, causing the camisole to cling to her breasts, which were of matronly size despite the blonde's otherwise youthful appearance.

Longarm stared in surprise as he slid his eyes from the pretty, mud-dappled blonde to the third freighter trudging through the hip-high water to stand beside the blonde and regard Longarm angrily, one fist on her slender hip.

The third freighter was no more of a man than the second one, though this one wore a man's oversized trail clothes—faded blue denims, green work shirt, and suspenders, with a shabby canvas hat perched on her pretty head. Her skin was darker than the blonde's, and her face was only lightly freckled.

Long, straight brown hair fell down from beneath her hat and behind her shoulders, blowing out slightly in the afternoon breeze.

"Pa asked you a question, mister?" she bit out, bunching her lips. "Who the fuck *are* you and what the fuck do you *want*?"

The blonde swallowed and said halfheartedly, her full, muddy breasts rising and falling heavily, "We're . . . armed!"

Longarm let his eyes sweep the girl's curvaceous frame. If she was armed, it had to be with a mighty small gun tucked up somewhere the sun never shone.

His bemusement left him, and he looked back at the bearded bulldog in the driver's boot. "There's three Injuns trailin' me, mister. And I have a feeling it isn't because they're lost. If there's three out here, there's more. And bogged down in a creek you never should have tried to cross in that heap isn't where you wanna be just now."

The bulldog craned his stout, lined neck to look behind him. Turning back to Longarm, he threw up an arm in anger. "What the hell you sittin' *there* for? Help us git 'em *out*!"

Longarm chuffed and heeled the pinto ahead, pulling the roan through the muddy, evenly flowing water. He rode up around the two girls—the brunette looked a few years older than the blonde, though neither was over twenty-five, he decided—and leaped down from his saddle and into the brisk, mud-bottomed stream. Muck from the bottom floated up to color the moving water around his knees a light chocolate tan.

Muttering curses, he glanced back to the other side of the stream. He and the freighting party would be in a fine fix if the Indians, turning out to be the kill-hungry renegades that he assumed they were, attacked them here. Grabbing his reata from his saddle, he went back and tied one end of the rope to the harness of the left front mule. He dallied a loop around the roan's neck before wrapping the other end around his saddle horn.

As he hauled himself back onto the pinto's back, he glanced at the bearded bulldog scowling at him impatiently from the wagon's driver's seat. "Put up that blacksnake and urge 'em gentle or you're on your own," he growled.

The bearded bulldog tightened his jaws as he reluctantly

wound the whip around the leather handle and set the handle in its tin socket near the brake lever.

Longarm turned forward. The two girls stepped wide of him and the wagon, trudging through the stream while eyeing the tall, steely-eyed newcomer skeptically. When they were safely out of the way, Longarm ground his boot heels against the pinto's ribs and pulled the roan up close beside him. Feeling the rope grow taut and begin to pull with the weight of both horses, the lead mule brayed and balked.

"Stubborn cayuse!" the skinner bellowed behind Longarm.

"Come on," Longarm urged the pinto, once more grinding his heels against the animal's ribs.

The horse lunged forward. So did the roan. Behind him, Longarm felt the mules put some slack into the rope. Then both nickered and brayed, and he heard the water gurgle as they started forward.

"That's the way, ya mangy critters!" the driver bellowed, flicking his reins across their backs. He laughed as the wagon started moving behind the mules, which were lumbering behind Longarm and the snorting, heaving horses.

Gradually increasing his speed as the mules gave themselves over to him, Longarm made the opposite side of the stream. As the horses clomped up onto the sandy shore, he ground his heels harder against the pinto's ribs, urging more speed for they had the low embankment yet to climb.

By the time they gained the sandy shore, however, the mules' pumps seemed to be primed, and the rope fell slack between Longarm's saddle and the left mule as the animals hauled the wagon with relative ease up the shallow embankment and onto the flat ground beyond.

Longarm glanced back with relief to see the wagon sitting safely atop the sage-stippled embankment, the mules looking owly but frisky as they shook their heads, twitched their ridiculous ears, and stomped as the stream's muddy water sluiced off their withers and down their stout, muscular legs.

"I'll be damned!" the bulldog cried, clambering down from the driver's boot and marching, bull-legged and poking his shapeless canvas hat back off his broad, freckled forehead, toward Longarm. "I thought I was gonna have to build a raft and send every bit of my freight downstream!"

Guffawing, the man stopped beside the pinto and stuck out a ham-sized hand as Longarm stepped down from the saddle. Giving the man's hand a halfhearted squeeze, he narrowed an eye. "Sometimes mules get spooked at the smallest thing—maybe a rabbit on the bank or a piece of driftwood goin' by. All it takes is a little encouragement to get 'em moving again. But if you lose your temper, they'll lose theirs and show you who's really boss. That's what happened out there."

Longarm was coiling his reata as the two girls climbed the bank behind the wagon, both, including the haughty-eyed brunette, looking relieved.

"You must know mules better'n me," the man said.

"Long time ago, I drove a hider's wagon pulled by a pair of Missouri mules like these," Longarm said. "I take it you ain't been skinnin' long."

"Nah," the bulldog said. "I was a farmer up Dakota way. Got snowed out, then dried out, and decided to come out here and haul supplies between mining camps. This is my first trip, don't ya know."

"I sorta figured it was."

The bulldog chuckled. "I'm Lin Lyndecker." He glanced behind him to where the two girls stood regarding Longarm shyly, the brunette running her hand along the neck of one of the mules. "These is my girls—Birt and Randi."

"Randi with an *i*," the brunette said.

"Same for Birt," Birt said.

"Ladies." Longarm pinched his hat brim, reflecting briefly on the decidedly unfeminine names for two such beautiful girls. "Custis Long." He frowned toward the other side of the stream where the three Indians, whom he could see more clearly now and who were indeed Ute braves, all three fairly young and wild-eyed, sat their horses at the water's edge.

Two of the horses drew water while another craned its neck to nip at the flies harassing its ass. Its rider—a tall, lean Indian clad in a brown vest, deerskin leggings, and high-topped mocassins, with a beaded medicine pouch dangling down his chest—held a Winchester carbine over his shoulder. There was a grim cast to his feral eyes as he stared at Longarm, his lips moving as he spoke to the others, who were also staring toward Longarm's side of the stream.

"Ah, shit," Lyndecker said. "I thought they was all supposed to be leashed to their reservations. That's what the man I'm workin' for over to Walsenberg told me."

"I got a feelin' those three didn't like being tied up," Longarm growled. He glanced at the girls. "You two best get in the wagon. We'll find a place to fort up till we find out what their intentions are."

As the girls and their father headed for the wagon, Longarm stepped into his saddle, his brows deeply furrowed. Alone, he could keep ahead of those renegades. But he couldn't leave the three inexperienced Lyndeckers to fend for themselves. The old granger and the pretty girls would be easy, irresistible pickings.

He booted the pinto forward, dallied the roan's lead line around his saddle horn, and used his free hand to shuck his Winchester from its saddle boot. He cocked the rifle one-handed and gigged the horses into a canter, looking around for high, protected ground somewhere ahead.

He had a feeling that he and the Lyndeckers were going to need it soon.

Chapter 8

Longarm brought a nickel cheroot to his lips and drew the smoke deep into his lungs. Exhaling the cheap but rich tobacco through his nostrils, he looked around the area he'd chosen for him and the Lyndeckers to fort up for the rest of the day and evening.

Frustration bit him. He wanted to be fogging the killers' trail, but here he was, holed up with a pugnacious old farmer turned mule skinner, wasting time.

There wasn't much else he could have done, however. He'd led the renegades—if the Utes were indeed running roughshod off their reserve—right to the stuck Lyndecker wagon. The least he could do was stay with the man and his daughters through the evening, in case the Utes made a play. If they were going to make a move, they'd likely do it soon. He'd light out for Cimarron again first thing in the morning.

The wagon sat up the slope a ways behind him, a spring rippling in a rocky hollow to its right. Beyond the wagon was a rocky knob jutting from the side of the fir-clad ridge. Below Longarm yawned a broad, sage-carpeted valley cut by several creeks, including the one in which the Lyndeckers had been mired. Beyond the valley floor, another fir-clad ridge rose steeply, the sky beyond darkening as the sun fell.

It was as good a spot with water as he could find on short notice, and it gave him a good view of the valley from which the Utes would have to come if they came.

Splashing and giggling sounded behind him. He glanced over his left shoulder to see the two Lyndecker girls, both clad now only in their underwear, splashing in the pool from the runoff spring.

The mules stood stonily behind them, knee-deep in the water, twitching their big ears as the girls, finished scrubbing the mud from the animals' hocks and withers, splashed each other and wrestled, squealing and laughing like sexy wood sprites who'd wandered down out of the spruce green forest rising behind them to play in the cool spring waters bubbling up from mossy stones.

The shoulder strap of the blonde's camisole slipped down her arm as she tried to dunk her sister's head beneath the rippling pool. One of her mud-dappled breasts—large and pear-shaped—sprang free of its inadequate tether to jostle freely. Laughing and shouting as she dunked her squealing sister, the blonde was oblivious.

Movement near the wagon raked Longarm's attention from the pool, and he turned to see the stocky, bearded Lyndecker ambling toward him from the cookfire he'd built. The man was smoking a corncob pipe, and a Patterson Colt that looked as ancient as its soft leather holster flapped down the front of his thigh.

Longarm glanced at the man's daughters again. Both the blonde's breasts were now free of the camisole as she and her sister fought and frolicked like nymphs in the pool. By force of will, Longarm turned his head to stare out over the valley, the tips of his ears warming with embarrassment as he heard the crunch of Lyndecker's boots in the grass and sage behind him.

"See anything out there, Marshal?"

"Nope," Longarm said, holding his gaze on the valley. He wondered if the man knew his daughter was virtually swimming naked a few dozen feet away from a complete stranger.

He sort of wished Lyndecker would make her stop, but only sort of.

Lyndecker chuckled as he dropped to a knee beside Longarm, looking out over the crest of the hill the two men were perched on. "Them girls o' mine . . ." He chuckled again. "They're used to livin' isolated-like. You know, in Dakota farm country. They'd cavort in their birthday suits in the stock troughs in the middle of the damn day. They never had a mother—not a *real* one anyways—and I never taught 'em no different 'cause there weren't another neighbor for two miles to the north, and he was an old Swede half blinded by some bad liquor he swilled in Fort Pierre!"

"Ya don't say," Longarm said, because he didn't know what else to say.

The man had no doubt seen him staring at his girls. It wasn't exactly a time for staring at naked girls. It wasn't a gentlemanly thing to do no matter what time it was nor how comely the girls' wares.

But what was he supposed to do when two frisky fillies were frolicking practically right in front of him?

"Well, I'll just have to ask you to ignore 'em," Lyndecker said. "They don't know no better, and it is right hard to change the habits you was born with."

Longarm only grumbled uncomfortably, squeezing his Winchester stock with one hand while he held the cigar to his lips with the other, taking another deep drag off his cheroot.

"No sign of the Utes," he said, exhaling smoke and changing the subject. "That doesn't mean they're not out there, but like as not they've drifted on. Injuns don't normally like a fight unless the odds are stacked in their favor. They probably saw how forted up we were, and that we were both armed, and decided to vamoose for easier prey."

"You think so?"

Lyndecker lay prone along the grassy slope, running a meaty hand through his chin whiskers as he studied the valley with wary eyes. Molasses-colored moles and yellow age spots marked his face; what appeared an old knife wound knotted and discolored the flesh beneath his frosty blue right eye, which sagged slightly in its socket.

"I don't know," Lyndecker continued. "Injuns scare the hell outta me—I don't mind sayin'. Had to put up with the smelly demons up Dakota way. Never got used to 'em. Me, I'd see an Injun, I'd shoot 'em. Now, I'm too old and stove up for fightin' them red devils alone."

He rolled his eyes up toward Longarm with a faintly desperate, beseeching cast. "I hope you'll stick around, Marshal. I sure would feel better havin' an extra gun guardin' the wagon and them girls o' mine. 'Specially one with your obvious experience and expertise."

Longarm shook his head. "No chance. I'm after a pack of curly wolves that make those three Utes look like choirboys. Every minute those killers are on the loose, there's a chance one more innocent soul will die at their bloody hands. I'm moving on in the morning."

"If it ain't them three we seen by the creek, it might be

three more," Lyndecker said. "Red renegades and like as not white ones, too. I didn't realize how woolly this country still was. You see, I gotta get this freight to Cimarron in three days, or I'll lose my job."

Longarm glanced at the man, who was staring up at him desperately. "Your boss should've hired outriders. At the very least, you should have left those girls to home."

"Nah," Lyndecker said, stretching his lips back from his teeth and returning his nervous gaze to the shadow-swept valley. "They go where I go. I don't trust 'em on their own." He chuffed mirthlessly. "Hell, I don't trust no men around 'em, and there's plenty o' them horny ranch men and greasers back in Walsenberg."

"Sorry, Lyndecker." Longarm prickled at the man's unreasonable request as well as at his own unfounded guilt. "You should have thought ahead. I'm pullin' out in the morning."

The bulldog narrowed an eye and stretched one side of his thin-lipped mouth wolfishly at the lawman. "I'll let ya lay with one—whichever one you want. She'll be all yours tonight."

Longarm stared at him blankly, not sure he could trust his ears.

"Sure," Lyndecker said. "I don't mind, as long as I know who's rollin' up with 'em. Big, strappin' hombre like you— hell, I'd be proud." He jerked his head back toward the pool where the girls continued to laugh and splash. "Which one?"

"You'd whore out your daughters to me?"

"Well, one of 'em." Lyndecker frowned, suddenly indignant. "Hell, it'd likely save their life!"

"Sorry, mister. Like I told you—those killers murdered an old friend of mine, and they're likely to do the same to others if they're not run to ground soon." Longarm had turned away from the man in disgust, but now he glanced back at him, cheeks flushed with fury. "Save yourself a few stitches and don't ask me again."

"I seen you starin' at 'em!" Lyndecker said accusingly.

Longarm narrowed his eyes as he took another drag off his cheroot, setting his jaws. "Starin's one thing."

Lyndecker's eyes had turned flat and malignant, kindling a raw, grinding anger. The discolored scar around his face turned white, its wrinkled edges bright red. "Then you stay away from 'em, hear? Don't you go near either one of 'em. Birt—she's got the coquette in her, that one. Just the same, you so much as try to squeeze her ass or nibble her neck"—the man pulled a wide-bladed bowie knife from the sheath at his hip and, laying the blade against his own forearm, showed its razor edge to Longarm—"and I'll gut you like a *pig!*"

Longarm's own hard gaze fell to the blade. Then his eyes rose slowly to Lyndecker's menacing glare. "Sheath that stick or swallow it," he said tautly, just loudly enough to be heard above the breeze.

He said nothing more.

Lyndecker stared back at him. Gradually, the menace ebbed from his eyes, replaced with a wary flatness. With a grunt, he slowly lowered the blade to his waist and shoved the bowie back down in its sheath. Then, continuing to stare back at Longarm with a mix of anger and caution, he pushed heavily to his feet, breathing hard through his broad nostrils, and tramped back down the hill to his wagon.

"Girls!" he shouted, throwing up an angry hand. "What the fuck're you doin' down there playin' like ya got no sense when there's supper to cook?" As he continued to stalk back toward the fire, he bellowed with echoing rage,

"Git to work or I'll take you both over my knee and wallop the holy hell outta your naked asses! Make you so sore you won't sit for a week!"

Longarm turned his gaze back to the valley, stuck the cheroot between his teeth, and loosed a caustic chuff around it. If it wasn't for the girls, he'd pull out and let Lyndecker fend for himself. A haircut by a Ute barber was just what the vitriolic old asshole needed.

Lyndecker didn't say anything to Longarm over the next couple of hours. Neither did the girls, whom the man had scolded into a testy silence as they cooked a pot of beans and side pork and made biscuits that, he pointed out with tooth-gnashing rage, were slightly burned on their bottoms.

Longarm didn't eat around the fire, deciding instead to take his supper a ways down the hill on a stone that he'd perched on before and that gave him a good view of the valley over which the high-country night was closing fast.

The western sky turned umber behind misty, silhouetted peaks. Shadows swept over the near piney ridges, and the breeze picked up, bringing the yammers of distant coyotes.

When he'd finished the beans and side pork and the two muffins Birt had slipped him with a little upward quirk of her wide, full mouth, he went back to the fire for more coffee. The brunette, Randi, was giving her father hell for farting.

"Well, goddamnit, you put too damn much o' them chili peppers in the beans," Lyndecker growled. He leaned back against a rock, a steaming coffee cup in his hand, a corked whiskey bottle leaning against his side.

"Did not," Randi said, taking Longarm's plate and fork and jerking her angry eyes at her father. "I put just as much chili in as I always do, and you never fart and complain the way you are now. You're just mad at *him*"—she hooked her thumb at Longarm, who was reaching down for the coffee-pot—"and takin' it out on *us!*"

Lyndecker scowled, his eyes suddenly tense with concentration. He lifted one hip and loosed a loud fart, the smell of which wafted like the stink of a fresh cow plop in the hot sun. The man laughed without mirth at his brunette-haired daughter. "There you go—there's one just for you, you little bitch. Christ, if you don't take after your ma . . . !"

Longarm poured himself a cup of coffee and turned to the pugnacious old bulldog sitting against his rock. "I'll take the first watch till midnight. Then you're up for two hours. I suggest you go light on that Who-Hit-John."

The man wrinkled his nose at Longarm, snarled, glared into his steaming cup, then swirled its contents, muttering to himself, and indulged in a liberal sip of his coffin varnish and coffee.

Longarm shouldered his rifle and, holding his coffee cup in his free hand, headed back into the night.

"Hey, Lawdog," one of the girls called to him.

He glanced back to see the full-figured blonde facing him from the rear of the wagon. The fire behind her silhou-etted her delightfully—the full breasts jutting proudly from beneath her shirtwaist. She had one fist on her hip, her head canted to one side, wavy blond hair falling over a shoulder.

"I know who you are," she said.

Longarm frowned.

She removed her fist from her hip and stomped toward him, swaying her hips provocatively under her plain gray dress. As she approached, he saw that she held something in her right hand. Stopping before him, she held up a thin, paper-covered book and slapped it against his chest.

"You're the one I read about in this here pamphlet," she said. "You're the Long Arm of the Law his ownself!"

"Let me see that."

He leaned his rifle against his leg and took the book from the girl. Holding it to the last of the light in the sky, he frowned down at the story she had it open to.

There was a caricature of him—a tall, gangly gent with a longhorn mustache, snuff brown hat, black frock, and string tie aiming a long-barreled revolver. The revolver was spewing smoke and flames, and the the nasty hombre on the other side of the page, who had a bag of apparently stolen loot over his shoulder and a stubby cigar clamped between his big teeth while aiming a shotgun, was tumbling straight back toward the bank behind him, pain etched on his ugly face.

Frightened onlookers peered out from the bank's small, square windows and its bullet-torn front door, one woman holding her face in her hands.

Above the illustration were the words in bold print: "CUSTIS P. LONG—THE LONG ARM OF THE LAW."

Below it, in smaller type: "THE FIERCEST LAWDOG WEST OF FORT SMITH ALWAYS GETS HIS MAN—ALIVE OR DEAD!"

Longarm chuckled. "I'll be damned. Heard about that. Truth be told, I don't remember ever shooting no bank robber just leaving a bank—leastways, none that looked like this hombre."

He lightly slapped the book against the girl's opulent chest. "And I wouldn't believe everything I read, Miss Birt. Someone asked to interview me for a couple of dime novel yarns, but I refused, so what you read in there was all based on hearsay. If the yarn spinner didn't just make it all up, that is—which he probably did."

"He didn't make it up about you bein' tall," the girl said, a little breathless, clutching the book to her breasts. "And . . . rugged-lookin' . . . if you don't mind me sayin', Longarm." She frowned. "You mind if I call you Longarm?"

"Most folks do." With that, Longarm pinched his hat brim and started to turn away.

"If you need anything later," the girl said urgently, taking another step forward, "I'll be right happy—"

"Birt!" Lyndecker called from the fire. "Birt, you get your skinny ass back here pronto, girl! You got dishes to wash and more coffee to make!"

The girl stared up at Longarm, looking pained.

"I said pronto!" Lyndecker shouted. "I need some liniment rubbed into my feet!"

"Good night, Miss Birt," Longarm said with a wry chuff, and ambled off into the night.

"Good night, Longarm." He could feel her staring at his back. Quickly, she added, "Birt's short for Birdelia, by the way!"

"Good night, Birdelia."

Chapter 9

Longarm took the first watch, then rousted Lyndecker for the second. When he heard the grizzled bulldog tramping back toward the wagon and the fire they kept burning low for coffee, he climbed up from his blanket roll and tipped the dented tin pot over his coffee cup.

Only a few watery grounds dripped out.

He filled the pot at the spring, and when he came back and set it on the fire, he jerked his head up suddenly as one of the girls cried sharply, "Git away from me, damn you! I told you, Papa, if you ever tried that again, I was gonna take my pigsticker to you!"

Then came an incoherent growl and a snarl, like that of a wolf that had been run off a trash heap. Then Longarm saw a shadow move beyond the fire, where Randi had rolled up on pine boughs beneath a fir tree.

"I was just tryin' to get a little warm from ya!" Lyndecker rasped, a blurry silhouetted image climbing out from under the girl's striped blankets, breathing hard.

"Git! Git!" The brunette gave the old man a hard shove, nearly knocking him down to his hands and knees.

"You little bitch!" Lyndecker pushed off his knees and, grunting, tramped back toward his own bedroll on the other side of the fire. "Heart cold as a snowmelt stream, I swear! Just like your damn ma!"

Randi gave a caustic grunt as she snuggled back down in her blankets. "I'll show you cold next time you try *warmin'* up to me!" She punched the flour sack she used for a pillow, then slammed her head down against it with another angry grunt.

"Sassy little bitch," Lyndecker growled as he lowered his heavy bulk to his own blankets. "You need the strap is what you need!"

As he lay down and drew up his blankets, Longarm saw Birt looking up from her own blanket roll, switching her gaze between her sister and father. She blinked as though half asleep, then shrugged, sighed, flopped back down, rolled over, and drew her blankets up over her head.

Longarm regarded the three with an incredulous scowl. A sweeter family he'd never known. He had a feeling if old Lyndecker tried "warming up" to one of his girls again, however, Randi would make good on her pigsticker threat.

The coffeepot chugged. He waited for it to boil, then threw in a handful of coffee. He let the water come back to another boil, then added a little cold water from his canteen to settle the grounds.

He filled his cup with the fresh, piping-hot brew, returned the pot to a rock just off the glowing coals, and cup in hand, rifle resting on his shoulders, tramped off to circle the camp, looking around and listening for wayward shadows and for unnatural noises rising above the faint bubbling of the nearby spring.

A couple hours later, having circled the camp a couple

of times slowly, stopping often to watch and listen, he threw down behind a fir tree near the wagon.

As it was only a couple of hours from dawn, he'd let Lyndecker sleep. He didn't want to have to bother with the old scalawag anyway. He'd doze for a few minutes at a time while keeping his ears open for the soft crunch of moccasined feet approaching in the bunchgrass and sage.

No Indian could move as silently as they were often given credit for, and those who said they could had never encountered an Indian anywhere except in dime novels like the one from which Birt had read about Longarm's own likely fictional exploits.

He was awakened from his last doze by a shrill scream. Lifting his head up from the fir log, heart racing, he looked around wildly, trying to get his bearings.

Dawn was a pearl wash above the piney eastern ridge, casting more murky shadows than light.

The scream rose, muffled this time. It was followed by a man's guttural cry. A sharp slap cut the dense morning silence, and Longarm jerked his head beyond the stream and along the edge of the firs dropping down the eastern ridge to see two scurrying shadows—one white, the other dark brown.

There was a dull yellow flash of Birt's jostling hair.

Longarm grabbed his rifle and heaved to his feet, racking a shell into the breech and glancing toward the white-covered wagon up the slope and at the edge of the trees behind him. Grumbling sounded as Lyndecker stirred, and then in the morning hush, Randi's voice was crisp and clear as she said, "What was that?"

As if in reply, a chortling sob sounded, and Longarm turned to see the brown figure bend at his knees and pull Birt—at least, what looked and sounded like Birt—over his shoulder. The man started to run along the line of trees across the shoulder of the sage-carpeted slope, sixty yards away and widening the gap between him and Longarm. The lawman snarled a curse, leaped the fir log, and took off running, holding the Winchester up high across his chest.

He glanced back toward the camp where Lyndecker was reaching for his rifle, and shouted, "Stay with the wagon!"

Longarm covered fifty yards quickly, racing up and over one low hummock after another. But he wasn't gaining much ground on the Indian until, angling toward a shadowy hollow on the downslope, Birt suddenly kicked free of his grasp. With another shrill cry, she hit the ground on her back, then jerked her angry face at the Indian and screamed, "Get your hands off me, you greasy savage!"

Longarm dropped to a knee and raised the Winchester to his shoulder. As the Indian grabbed the girl's arm and jerked her brutally toward him, Longarm lined up the rifle's sights on the brave's deerskin-clad chest, which shone with beadwork in the wan light.

In the corner of his eye, a shadow flicked to his right and only about ten yards away. He held fire on the Indian's chest and flung himself to the left a quarter second before a rifle cracked close by. He saw the flash as he hit the ground and rolled, the bushwhacker's slug blowing up dust and gravel behind him.

It was followed by another crack and flash about ten feet to the left of it, and Longarm squeezed his eyes closed as gravel peppered his face. As the metallic rasp of a cocking lever sounded, he rolled over a spine of rock and down a slight depression.

Three more rifle blasts peppered the rocky ridge, flinging stone in all directions.

Again, Birt screamed angrily. Behind Longarm, Lyndecker shouted and distant rifles popped—at least two guns, maybe three.

Heart hammering—shit, the Ute braves must have doubled in number—Longarm ran crouching to his left behind the shallow depression. The Utes shouted something in their guttural tongue as, laughing and jeering, they fired six more rounds at the rocky lip.

They were now firing behind Longarm.

The lawman snarled an enraged curse and bounded back up and out of the lip. He sprinted forward across flat ground, then leaped into the depression in which the two bushwhacking braves were hunkered twenty yards to his right. One was looking over the top of the ridge, toward where Longarm had disappeared a minute ago, while the other fed cartridges into his Winchester carbine from the two belts crisscrossed on his bony waist.

Longarm didn't warn them that he had them dead to rights.

They hadn't warned *him*.

He cut loose with a short hail of lead into both, then, glimpsing them both twisting, falling, and throwing their rifles as they died, took off running again toward the brave that had nabbed Birt. He couldn't see either the girl or the Indian, but he continued running in the direction they'd been headed before he'd been so rudely interrupted.

He'd just run up from a low draw when a horse bounded out of the draw close ahead.

The Indian sat his blanket saddle, crouched over the blonde draped across the horse's withers in front of him. She grunted loudly as the cream mustang hammered violently onto the lip of the draw and started across the shoulder of the slope, angling toward the valley.

The Indian's hair, shiny with bear grease and braided

with rawhide, flopped down his broad back, as did the carbine hanging by a leather lanyard. His elbows flapped like wings as he ground his moccasins against the mustang's ribs.

Longarm stopped, raised the Winchester, aimed quickly, and fired.

The whip-crack of the rifle echoed around the slope, sounding like a cannon blast in the early morning quiet.

The echo was only beginning to die when the Indian sagged forward and to his right, the rifle sliding off his shoulder and hitting the ground. He straightened, sagged again more sharply, threw an arm toward his horse's mane, missed it, and tumbled down the mustang's right side.

The Indian hit the ground and rolled down a grade and out of sight. The horse and the girl dropped out of sight down the same grade.

The girl screamed. The horse whinnied. Hooves clomped loudly.

Longarm sent the spent cartridge smoking over his shoulder, racked fresh, and set out running once again. He'd run ten yards when the riderless mustang reappeared once more, lunging up from the other side of the ravine into which the girl and the Indian had apparently fallen.

Longarm's breath was coming hard, raking his lungs, when he finally pushed through a thin stand of gnarled cedars and stunted cottonwoods, stopped at the lip of the steep-walled ravine, and looked down. The girl lay on the gravelly bottom, her dress, caught on the short branch of a sun-bleached log, hiked up to the small of her back to reveal her pale, round, naked ass.

Longarm swept his eyes up and down the ravine, frowning with befuddlement. There was no sign of the Indian.

The blonde rose up onto her elbows and, swiping at her

dress to free it, rolled onto her back—dusty, dazed, and disheveled. Holding his rifle in both hands across his chest, Longarm started moving sideways down the steep bank.

The girl's eyes dropped to Longarm's side of the cutbank, and widened in shock. *"Look out, Lawdog!"*

Something reached out as if from the earth itself to grab Longarm's ankle, tripping him. With a surprised grunt, the lawman tumbled straight forward, instinctively releasing the rifle and throwing out his hands as the bottom of the cut rose up in a flash to wallop his right shoulder and hip.

"No!" the girl cried as the lawman, grunting and snarling, rolled onto his back, gritting his teeth against the pain sparking through him.

The Indian gave a wild, tooth-gnashing whoop as he bounded out from where he'd crouched against the cutbank's recessed wall. Blood matted the obsidian hair at the side of his head where Longarm's forty-four slug had grazed him. A knife blade flashed in his right fist as he dived straight forward, teeth bared, tea brown eyes bright with fury.

Longarm thrust his left hand up, catching the wrist of the bounding Indian's right hand when the curved tip of the razor-edged blade was only six inches from his throat. The Indian, sprawled atop him, squirmed and wriggled like a snake, grinding against Longarm and pushing down on the blade with savage, snarling fury.

Longarm watched the blade drop farther. When he felt the point nip the skin like the sting of an angry hornet, he jerked his right arm up from beneath the savage's left shoulder, and wrapped that hand, too, around the Indian's wrist, pushing up.

The Indian bunched his chapped, pink lips, and his eyes bulged from their sockets as he continued thrusting down.

Longarm removed his right hand from the Indian's right wrist, and just as the point of the knife touched his throat once more, he brought his right fist back, cocked it, and smashed it soundly against the Indian's face. The Indian's head snapped sideways with a surprised chuff. His hand released the knife.

Longarm rolled and kicked, thrusting the Ute to one side. Shaking his head as if to clear it, the brave scrambled quickly on all fours away from Longarm, knowing he was suddenly on the defensive, but gradually gaining his feet.

He wheeled to face the lawman, crouching, eyes wild, blood trickling now from the four-inch line of split skin on his right cheek.

Losing track of the knife, Longarm heaved himself up. Just as he squared his feet to face the brave, his opponent lunged ahead and right, thrusting his hand toward the rope-handled bowie half-buried in dirt and gravel. The brave had scooped the knife two feet off the ground, when Longarm lunged forward and kicked the brave's wrist.

The Ute gave an enraged cry as the knife sailed up and careened backward, hitting the ravine's floor with a metallic clatter and scrape. Gritting his teeth, he lunged forward and swung a haymaker up from his knees.

Longarm ducked under the savage blow and laid a left-right combination against the brave's solar plexus. The brave staggered backward, slumping forward. Longarm gave the Indian a taste of his own medicine with a haymaker that started from the heels of his scuffed cavalry boots and ended with a snapping, cracking, popping sound against the Indian's left jaw hinge.

"Gnahhh!" the brave screamed as he staggered backward and sideways, the entire side of his face losing its color.

Before the brave could fall, Longarm grabbed the front of the brave's vest in both hands, held him upright, and head-butted him. As the Ute became a deadweight in his arms, the lawman twisted him around and, still clutching the brave's beaded vest in both fists, ran him across the arroyo and smashed him head first against the solid, eroded ravine wall.

There was a grating crack, and the back of the Ute's neck bulged, broken.

"*Oaff . . .*" the brave grunted.

Longarm released him.

He fell straight down to the arroyo's sandy floor, expiring with one last gurgling exhalation and a fart. Above him, there was a deep indentation in the shape of his forehead in the arroyo's root-webbed, bone-flecked wall.

Longarm backed away from the dead Indian, clutching his throbbing right fist. He let his marbles roll back into their rightful sockets and, when he'd caught his breath, turned to his left.

The blonde, Birt, stood several yards away, staring at him slack-jawed. Slowly, she shook her head, eyes wide with awe. "That writer fella—that Mr. Dead-Eye Dick—he has you down *pat*!"

Longarm brushed sand and clay from the torn sleeve of his frock coat and glowered at the pretty blonde. "What in the hell were you doing so far from camp?" He doubted the Indian would have dragged her that far without her sounding an alarm.

The girl bunched her lips in sudden anger, and thrust an arm toward the wagon. "I was off tendin' nature, away from Pa and his sneaky—!"

A rifle cracked in the direction of the camp, interrupting Birt and clearing the remaining cobwebs from behind Long-

arm's grit-laden eyes. He staggered forward, picked up his
hat, and mashed it weakly onto his head. As another rifle
crack flatted out across the slope, he grabbed his Winchester and, brushing it off, scrambled, huffing and puffing and
levering himself with small cedars, up the arroyo's steep
wall.

"Stay here, Birt," he called behind him when he'd
gained the rim and started running toward the camp. "I'll
call you when it's clear!"

"Whatever you say, Longarm!"

It was a long run back, up and down the cuts bleeding
out from the fir-carpeted slope, and mostly uphill. He was
weak with exhaustion when he finally approached the wagon
from downslope, crouched over his Winchester and looking
around for more Indians.

He spotted two bodies crumpled on the ground about
fifty and seventy yards beyond the wagon, in a V-shaped
clearing stretching up into into the fir forest. Two blanket-
saddled mustangs grazed another hundred yards off, their
paint hides showing clearly now as the high-country light
intensified.

Longarm stopped and looked around. There was only
the wagon and, a little farther up the slope, the mussed bedrolls and the fire ring that sent up two feeble curls of gray-
blue wood smoke. No sign of Randi and Lyndecker.

"Goddamnit!" a man shouted. *"Fuck!"*

Longarm stepped around the wagon. On the other side
of it and twenty yards away from it, near a lone boulder
grown up with brush, Lyndecker lay on his side. He was
clad in only his baggy duck trousers, grimy undershirt, and
suspenders. He wore no boots, only socks from which several dirty toes protruded.

Randi knelt beside him, leaning on a Springfield carbine, both facing the two dead Indians farther off across the shoulder of the slope.

As Longarm approached, Randi glanced at him over her shoulder, her expression somber.

"Any more Injuns out there?" Longarm asked.

The girl shook her head, slowly blinked her brown eyes, then turned back to her father writhing on the ground before her. Longarm moved around her and looked down at Lyndecker.

The man lay with one arm draped over a rock. He held both hands clutched to his belly, but neither hand was visible amidst the blood and viscera spilling out around the Ute war lance protruding from his middle.

The dyed hawk feathers tied with rawhide to the end of the lance fluttered in the chill dawn breeze.

"Christ," Longarm said, dropping to one knee beside the bearded bulldog. "They got you good, didn't they?"

"I'll say they got me good!" the man grated out through clenched teeth, his furred cheeks balled with misery. He glanced down at the lance sticking out from just above his belly button, then looked at Longarm beseechingly. "You think there's any chance you could . . . ?"

Longarm shook his head. "Not without pulling everything left inside you out along with it."

Longarm heard grass crunch behind him, and jerked a wary glance over his shoulder, ready to bring his Winchester up. Birt moseyed toward them. He'd told her to wait in the draw, but his annoyance ebbed. Her old man had only a few minutes left.

She stood beside Longarm and, clutching her shoulders, frowned with only slight concern down at Lyndecker. "What the hell happened, Papa?"

Lyndecker snapped his head up at her, gritting his teeth

with pain and anger. "What the fuck you think happened, Birt? Can't you see the fucking war lance that's pinning me to the goddamn ground? You think I'm down here studying wildflowers or ants or some such bullshit as *that*?"

Longarm didn't see the Springfield muzzle drop toward the side of the man's head until after he'd heard the *k-pow!* Lyndecker's head jerked violently, and then the man removed his bloody hands from the bloody mess at his belly. His eyes flickering like dying lamp flames, his head sagged to the ground.

His cheek came to rest in a small, dusty sage shrub. He puffed a lone, expiring breath.

His legs kicked spasmodically. Then he lay still.

Longarm glanced in shock at Randi.

The brunette lifted the smoking barrel of her Springfield carbine and, angling her brown-eyed gaze down toward Lyndecker, shook her head sadly. "Poor Papa," she sighed. "He was suffering so."

Longarm turned stiffly to watch her and her sister walk arm in arm back toward the camp, Birt sobbing with negligible sorrow into a wrinkled hankie.

Chapter 10

Longarm buried Lyndecker while the girls made breakfast and chattered festively amongst themselves, as though it were the Fourth of July and they'd be dancing with their beaus that evening.

They even refused to lay the old reprobate to rest until after they'd eaten, washed the dishes, and rolled up their blankets.

Both tried to look appropriately glum—they weren't good enough actresses to feign anything close to bereavement—but Longarm sensed a definite buoyancy in their demeanors even as Randi read a few words from the old man's leather-bound Bible over his freshly mounded grave. The brightness in their eyes and barely restrained merriment bespoke a couple of schoolgirls about to start their first day of summer vacation, or two fourteen-year-old Texas cowboys ready to head out on their first cattle drive.

Longarm didn't begrudge them their covert grins and snorts and the decidedly louder, freer pitch of their conversations even while only discussing whether to throw out the beans or save them for that night's supper. He doubted either one of them had a gone a day without being castigated by the old bastard, or worse.

While packing up Lyndecker's possibles as Longarm hitched the horses to the covered wagon, Birt held up the old man's liniment bottle to Randi, her blond brow arched cunningly. The brunette pursed her lips, lowered her chin shrewdly, and nodded.

Biting her upper lip with concentration, Birt swung the bottle back behind her shoulder, then flung it up the slope and into the forest. The corked brown bottle flashed once in the mid-morning light, then disappeared amongst the branches, setting a squirrel to scolding.

The force of the throw caused Birt's low-cut summer blouse to drop down off her shoulders, exposing her large, pale breasts. Apparently, she wasn't given to donning underwear even up this high in the chill mountains. Chuckling with her sister, she gave Longarm a devilish grin.

His face warming in spite of his having known a good dozen Birt Lyndeckers in his eventful life, the lawman abruptly though begrudgingly turned away to resume tightening buckles and adjusting hames.

The Utes' skewering of their father might have been a fortuitous event for the Lyndecker girls, but it was the opposite of that for Longarm. Determined to finish hauling the mining supplies and sundry dry goods to Cimarron and collect the two hundred dollars for which the freight company in Walsenberg had contracted their father, Randi and Birt turned a deaf ear when the lawman mentioned they might be better off turning the wagon around and heading back to where they'd come from.

"You go on, Lawdog," Birt had said when she'd climbed into the driver's boot and unwound the reins from the brake handle. "We'll be all right."

Longarm swung up onto his paint's back, and looked at her. She was grinning under the brim of her man's over-large felt hat. Sitting beside her in the driver's boot, her sister smiled, canted her head to one side, and narrowed a pretty brown eye. They were daring him to abandon them to more renegade Utes and to all the other potential trail traps between here and Cimarron.

Impatience and anger raked Longarm. It seemed that the gods were conspiring to keep him from running down the killers of the lawmen and Richard Collins. But there was nothing he could do. If he left the two Lyndecker girls to their own devices, he'd feel just as wretched as he did now, feeling the killers slipping away from him like a wet raw-hide rope through his hands.

He scouted the trail and led the way along what ap-peared to be an old, abandoned stage road, and he pushed the girls and the horses hard, not stopping until nearly dark that night. They holed up along a cottonwood-sheathed stream in a broad valley, and the girls set up camp while he tended the horses, and coyotes sang in the darkening hills.

After supper, good dark came down, and Longarm poured himself a fresh cup of coffee. As he did, he noticed Birt watching him over her kettle of steaming wash water. She quirked a smile, blushing, then lifted the strap of her dress back up onto her bare shoulder, and turned back to the pan she'd been scrubbing.

"You'd best throw a coat on," Longarm suggested. "It gets cold up here of an evening."

"Ah, hell," Birt said, giving him a coquettish sidelong look, her blond curls pasted to her forehead by the water's steam. "I got hot blood running through my veins, Lawdog. Why, back home in Dakota I slept in the raw most nights, even in the middle of a plains winter!" She turned to Randi, who was pouring pinto beans into a pot to soak for the next day. "Didn't I, Sis?"

"Birt, you just mind your chores!" Randi scolded her.

As she continued scrubbing the pan, Birt kept her eyes on Longarm, spreading her wide, red lips. "Don't mind her. She's just owly sometimes."

Longarm was nettled by the heat the girl fairly radiated. He needed to keep his mind on the killers and not on the two comely waifs he'd found himself so inadvertently escorting to Cimarron.

Blowing on his coffee, he turned away, grumbling, "You two best turn in. We won't be losing any daylight come mornin'."

He kept watch from a rock above the creek, about fifty yards from the encampment. The position afforded him a broad, uninterrupted view of the valley over which stars sparkled like fresh snow. It was so quiet he could hear the rustle of a night bird's wings a half a mile away, and the faint scratching of a pack rat in the brush on the other side of the stream that glistened below him and between the dark cottonwoods like a large, black snake.

He'd strolled up and down the bank like a sentry walking the stockade wall of an army fort in Indian country, and had just sat on the rock again, when a soft feminine voice said, "Marshal Long?"

He glanced over his shoulder at the riverbank. A slender silhouette climbed the game path slanting up from the cottonwoods. It had to be Randi. Birt either called him Longarm or Lawdog, like she was a fictional heroine talking to a fictional hero in one of the dime novels she read by the dozens when Randi was taking a turn driving the wagon.

"Don't shoot me," the brunette said, a little breathless

but with an ironic edge in her voice as she continued up the bank.

Longarm rose and rested his Winchester across his shoulder. He anxiously rolled his lit cheroot from one side of his mouth to the other.

"What's wrong?" He hadn't heard anything untoward, but he couldn't catch everything in this big, open country between mountain ranges. He figured they were in the Uncompahgre Country, with the Black Canyon of the Gunnison River just north, but this far off the beaten path he wasn't sure.

She took long strides as she gained the lip of the bank. Longarm saw that she was clad in a buffalo robe. Her pale, bare feet protruded from beneath the heavy, musty garment that came down to her bare shins.

"Whew!" she said buoyantly, taking a deep breath. "That's a climb."

"Especially barefoot. You're like to step on a cactus or yucca plant, goin' around without shoes."

"I hardly ever wear shoes." Randi stopped before him, her straight, dark brown hair winging behind her in the vagrant night breeze. Below and behind her, the stream winked in the starlight. "I reckon it was how I was raised."

Longarm offered a wry grin around his cheroot. "Like ole Birt sleepin' in the raw?"

"I wanted to talk to you about that. About Birt, I mean."

"Oh?"

She glanced at Longarm's flat rock. "May I sit down?"

Longarm gestured to the rock, and when the girl had seated herself, holding the robe closed as she crossed her arms on her chest and planted one pale, bare foot atop the other, he sat down beside her.

He puffed the cheroot and stared straight out across the broad, treeless valley, toward a mountain range—one of several out here—humping darkly in the northeast. "So what it is about Birt you wanted to talk to me about?"

The girl fidgeted around on the rock. She sort of lowered her head between her shoulders, then lifted her chin and took a deep breath of the fresh, pinyon-scented air, as though calling up the words she was looking for. "My sister, Marshal Long, reads books and such. You know how she does."

"And I don't hold it again her neither, as long as she doesn't believe everything she reads."

"Well, that's the problem. Birt sorta does believe everything. She has a...uh...romantic way of lookin' at things. Yeah, that's the word. Me—I have a practical sense. When I look at a man, I see the man before me instead of the one all hazed out in make-believe."

Longarm looked down at the girl. "You're gonna have to chew this a little finer for me, Miss Randi. I'm not sure what you're getting at."

"Oh, I think you are." She looked at him, swinging her hair out behind her, an accusatory tone in her voice. "You know how she looks at you. Hell, you've become her knight in shining armor."

"Well, if you're suggesting that I'm gonna take advantage—"

"I'm just asking you, Marshal Long, to please remember that my sister is a very fanciful and innocent girl. She never got out as much as me back home in Dakota. I used to go to town and such with Papa, and sneak off to dances nights when he got drunk and passed out early. My sister pretty much stayed to the farm and, between chores, hunkered down in the shade of a haystack to read trashy novels by

Mr. Scott and those obscene plays of that Shakespeare fella."

"No kiddin'?" Longarm said. "I knew she read them dime novels, but I never realized she stooped to the likes of Shakespeare."

Randi stood and faced him from only a foot away. "My meaning here is this. I know you're a man, Marshal Long. With a man's goatish need. So, if you'll be requiring one of us in payment for guiding us to Cimarron"—with that, she dropped the buffalo robe down off her shoulders, letting it sag to her waist, exposing her breasts—"that one should be me."

Longarm's breath caught in his throat. Randi's breasts weren't quite as large as her sister's, but they were firm, smooth, and nearly perfectly round, and not one bit displeasing to a man's eye.

He let his incredulity show in his face. "You're . . ."

"Offering myself to save my sister," Randi finished for him, turning her head to one side in shame, but leaving her breasts fully exposed.

The wind blew strands of her brunette hair around her forehead and long, tan neck. Coyotes called from the velvety black hills and mountains behind her.

Longarm glanced at the exposed, slowly rising and falling bosoms once more, then at the girl's profile, her eyes downcast, waiting.

These Lyndecker girls were one surprise after another. He covered a chuckle by clearing his throat.

Standing, he lifted the robe back up over her shoulders and drew it across her breasts. She frowned up at him, shocked and maybe even a little indignant.

"That's mighty brave of you, Miss Randi. But I reckon I can keep the leash on my goatish need till we get to Cimar-

ron. I hear there's a couple nice whorehouses thereabouts."
He gave the girl a wink as he grabbed his rifle from beside
the rock. "Reckon I'll take another stroll around. You best
get on back to camp. Looks like you're catching a chill."

As he walked away, he could feel her eyes on his back.
It might have been the creek lapping over a rock, but he
thought he heard her give an angry chuff.

Chapter 11

Longarm had noticed horse tracks on the old stage road that he and the girls were following across the sage flats between mountain ranges. But he saw no horses until mid-morning of the day after Randi had offered herself to him on the night-cloaked creek bank.

He reined the pinto to a halt in the middle of the trace and stared off the trail's right side, where a white-socked dun stood near a clump of willows with its saddle hanging down its left side, the blanket roll tied to the cantle hung up in skunk cabbage.

"What is it, Longarm?" Birt called when Randi had halted the wagon behind him.

Raking his eyes across the flat up to the long hogback rising behind it, he spied another horse about a hundred yards beyond the first.

"You two stay here," he said, glancing over his shoulder at the two girls squinting at him from under their shading hands, the wagon's sunlit dust sifting around them.

Longarm booted the pinto off the trail and into a canter.

When he approached the dun, the horse turned toward him, whinnied, and edged away, dragging the blanket roll.

Then Longarm, swinging his gaze back and forth across the ground, spied something about forty yards to the left of the horse and slightly ahead of it. He rode over, dismounted, and knelt beside the dead man lying facedown in the sage.

The corpse wore a brown corduroy shirt under a spruce green brush jacket, checked trousers, and bull-hide chaps. On his red-topped boots, he wore large-roweled Chihuahua spurs.

There were two bloody bullet holes through the back of his jacket, and by the amount of flesh that had been blown out around his spine, he'd been shot from the front. Probably in ambush. The soft leather holster riding high on his left hip was empty, as had been the rifle scabbard on the dun.

His back was humped up because he was lying on a rock, and his legs were spread. Flies and ants had found the grisly red swath across the top of his head that marked where his hair had been before being hastily removed by a dull knife.

The blood was the texture of strawberry jelly. The man had been shot and carved up only a couple of hours ago.

All around between the sage and skunk cabbage were moccasin prints as well as the marks of unshod hooves.

Longarm stepped into the pinto's saddle and rode over toward the other horse. He was only halfway there when the pinto nickered. Looking around, Longarm saw a dark figure leaning back in the scant shade of a small, lone cottonwood just ahead and to his right.

He rode over and swung down from the saddle.

The man's face beneath his floppy-brimmed sombrero was bearded and angular, with two blue eyes staring out from windburned and sunburned sockets. He wore a checked shirt, pinto vest, and chaps over faded blue denims with blown-out leg seams. Blood matted his vest and his upper right thigh.

As Longarm approached, he stopped with a start when the man blinked. His eyes were like two blue lights in the cottonwood's scant shade.

Longarm set his hand on the walnut grips of his cross-draw .44. "You two part of the bunch that robbed the Silver-jack payroll?"

The man beneath the cottonwood blinked again. His darkly tanned throat moved as he swallowed. His lips parted and stretched a grim smile. "I hid up in them rocks yonder. Confounded the damn Utes. That's how I kept my hair."

Longarm frowned and turned his ear toward the dying man, whose voice was barely audible above the hot, dry breeze. He took another step forward. "You hear me?"

The man just stared at him, his face expressionless. Longarm guessed he wasn't much over eighteen, if that. The lawman hunkered down in front of him.

"What's your name, son?"

"Colby." His voice, pitched like a rusty hinge, was somewhere between a boy's and a man's.

"Where you from?"

"Ogallala."

"Still got folks there?"

Colby shook his head weakly. "Done broke with my folks near two summers ago."

Longarm sighed and pulled at a bunchgrass clump. Like so many, the kid had likely joined a trail drive, and then a group of misfits who'd convinced him there were easier ways than eating dogie dust to make a buck.

"Headin' for Cimarron?"

The kid's young eyes hardened slightly, and one cheek twitched in a wince as pain shot through him.

"Thought so." Longarm returned the kid's hard stare. "Where are the other two you were riding with? I saw four sets of tracks. How many are there total?"

The kid parted his lips but it took him nearly a half a minute to rake out, "There were twelve before we split up. And you can bet they'll send you to hell, you son of a bitch."

"Come on, Colby. You're dying. Time to set things right."

The kid's right nostril curled, and he tried to spit at Longarm, but managed only a small spurt of blood down his lower lip. Then his chest fell still and his eyes, still staring at Longarm, simply lost the light behind them. The blood on his lip glistened in the sunlight pushing between the cottonwood's spindly branches.

"Shit," Longarm said, looking around the sage flat, which was interrupted here and there with a willow or cottonwood or chokecherry patch. The Indians appeared to be doing his job for him. Trouble is, they were likely to run him and the girls down, too.

He hoped he caught up to the gang before the Utes caught up to him. He was too much a lawman to have decided with anything except the backside of his brain that he wasn't out here on official business.

He was on the gun trail, with a note to collect on the murder of an old friend.

He'd try to arrest as many of the gang as he could, of course. Again, he was too much of a lawman not to at least try to follow the book. But he'd have bet gold dollars to doughnuts there'd be damn few he wouldn't be hauling back to Grand View tied belly down across their saddles.

The prospect quickened his blood. Leaving the kid and the other dead man to the coyotes, he quickly ran down their horses, unsaddled and turned them loose, then galloped back to where the girls had pulled their wagon into the shade of a cabin-sized boulder.

Randi was watering the mules from her hat while Birt sat in the driver's boot, running a damp cloth down the front of her dress.

"More Injun sign," the lawman said, trying not to look at where Birt was running that cloth. "I'll stay back with the wagon. Keep your eyes peeled. You see anything, give a holler."

"You'll get us through to Cimarron, Longarm," Birt said, lifting a bare foot onto the Conestoga's dashboard. She poured a little water from her canteen down the front of her low-cut shirtwaist, making the cloth cling to her breasts. "I know you will."

Longarm sighed and rode away.

" 'I know you will,' " Randi mocked her sister behind him, loud enough for Longarm to hear. "Christalmighty, girl. Quit moon-calfin' around that man, will ya? He's so old and stove up, I'd bet gold nuggets to cow pies he couldn't get a hard-on for all the pussy in Colorado!"

They nooned for a half hour before fogging the trail again.

It was eerie, Longarm thought, how they didn't run into anyone out here. There was plenty of ranch land out this way, and he'd spied cattle grazing the high, grassy slopes along the Sawatch and the Iron Hills, but he spied no riders. Not even the distant rise of a dust plume.

They passed a couple of abandoned mine shacks near humped ore tailings, and an old, adobe brick rancho that had long been given back to the sage, but again, no people.

They watered the mules and Longarm's horses, one or the other of which he tied to the back of the wagon, at a spring bubbling up near the ruined casa, then continued through a sun-blasted valley between high, pine-clad peaks.

One of the mules came up lame around three in the afternoon, and Longarm looked around for a place to hole up and tend the beast's right front hock, from which he'd pulled a long cactus thorn. If the leg wasn't wrapped with mud and whiskey or turpentine, and then rested for a few hours, it would swell up, and then Longarm and the girls would really be in a fix.

As it was, they'd lose three hours of prime travel time. He ground his teeth with frustration, and cursed his luck once again for having run into the Lyndeckers, pretty as the girls were. Around three thirty, riding around from behind a broad, high-walled mesa, he reined the pinto to a halt, and touched his Colt's grips.

Ahead lay what appeared to be a stage relay station—a long, low lodge with a corral, a stable, and a barn sitting in the brush near a creek off to the left. The place was fronted by a windmill and a stock tank. There was a long porch running along the front wall of the lodge. Roofed with sun-bleached pine saplings, the porch offered cool, blue shade. A water jug hung from the rafters, a gourd dipper poking up from it.

There was no one about, no horses in the corral, and the lodge's windows were shuttered against the hammering sunlight. The only sounds were the sifting, dry breeze, buzzing flies, and cicadas.

The station looked abandoned. The dusty ground in front of it—as far as Longarm could tell from sixty yards away anyway—showed no recent horse tracks.

He rode back, stopped the wagon, and ordered the girls

to wait till he called for them. Then he turned the pinto around and cantered into the station yard, looking around and scouring the ground for horse tracks.

As he came around the corral, he checked the pinto down to a walk. Then, when his eyes spied a fresh, shod horse print in the mud around the base of the stock tank, he drew back sharply on his reins.

He'd no sooner touched his Colt's grips than something hot seared across the outside of his right thigh, and a rifle cracked sharply.

The pinto whinnied and pitched and, grabbing his rifle from the saddle scabbard, Longarm let himself roll off the horse's left hip. He hit the ground beside the stock tank as another rifle cracked from the direction of the lodge.

The pinto bugled an enraged whinny and, humping its back, wheeled and galloped off across the dusty yard to Longarm's left, hooves thumping loudly, reins trailing behind it.

Racking a shell into the Winchester's breech, hearing more shots cracking from the lodge and smashing into the rock-walled stock tank, Longarm hunkered down behind the tank. When the firing ceased, he raised the Winchester over the top of the tank and the black, hay-flecked water within, and snapped off four quick shots.

The slugs pounded the adobe lodge around the two front windows—one on each side of the door and from which the shutters had been thrown back. One bullet spanged off the iron shutter latch, and it must have grazed someone inside because Longarm heard a loud, enraged squeal.

Longarm ejected the spent brass and, before the echoes of his shots had died, he hoofed it at a dead run out from behind the stock tank and behind an adobe springhouse. Beyond were cedars and rocks and broken ground. Longarm continued running into the scrub to the right of the lodge.

The rifles resumed cracking furiously from the station house. A couple shots clipped rocks and scrub trees around Longarm's boots. Then he dropped into a dry creek bed, and the shooters lost him.

As he scrambled along the bottom of the arroyo, which meandered about fifty yards out from the east side of the lodge and was sheathed in shrubs, a few small cotton-woods, aspens, and pines, the shooters took a couple of potshots, but they landed far wide.

As he drew toward the back of the lodge, edging an occasional look over the arroyo's eroded, root-gnarled lip, he could hear the men from the lodge shooting probing shots behind him and whooping and hollering angrily.

The arroyo climbed into pines behind the lodge. When he was out of view of the lodge's side windows, Longarm scrambled up the side of the arroyo and ran straight out away from it until he was directly behind the lodge.

There was a door in the back wall, under a small porch roof. A window, boarded up from the outside, lay about ten feet to the right of the door. A corrugated tin tub, rusted through in places, hung on a nail beside the door. Over the door hung a rack of bleached deer antlers.

As another shot rang out from the east side of the lodge, gray smoke puffing, Longarm sleeved sweat from his brow, drew a deep breath, and ran out from the pines and down the rocky slope. He gained the back door just as footsteps pounded toward it from inside.

A man was yelling, ". . . if you hadn't gone and started shooting when he was still two miles from the front door!"

"Fuck you, Hoot!" the man near the back door shouted.

"I told you, I didn't mean to shoot. My goddamn finger twitched!"

Longarm pressed his back against the wall beside the door. There was the scrape of a locking bar being removed from its brackets.

The man farthest from the door shouted, "I shoulda known better'n to pair up with the likes of a damn fool. You *and* your brother Clifford. A couple o' damn fools from Julesburg!"

"You shut up about him, you heartless son of a bitch! He's *dead*!" The door scraped open as the man opening it said in a quaking voice, "Poor bastard was kilt by Utes, and you didn't even let me take the time to—"

Just as his flat, unshaven face appeared in the crack between the door and the door frame, Longarm bounded onto the stoop, smashing the butt of his Winchester through the opening.

The brass butt plate caught the man's forehead with a loud, crunching smack. It sounded like a pumpkin dropped on a stone floor.

The man went walleyed. He staggered straight back, dropping his rifle. Longarm thrust the door wide and bulled into the lodge. The man he'd beaned hit the floor on his back, and dust puffed from the earthen floor around him.

Longarm leaped over him, raising his rifle just as a man standing at the front window left of the front door wheeled, his straw sombrero tumbling off his head and down his back. He had long hair and a spade beard.

He gritted his teeth as he raised his Spencer repeater, but before he could bring it to bear, Longarm fired three quick shots from a crouch, boots spread a shoulder width apart.

The blond gent screamed and flew straight back out the

front window. His knees hung up on the ledge, and he hung there, half in and half out of the lodge. His boots flopped, and his spurs grated into the adobe beneath the window.

Longarm heard him strangling as he hung down the front wall. Striding toward the front of the room, swinging his rifle left and right across the long, low-ceilinged station house, wary of more bushwhackers, he glanced over the window ledge.

The blond gent's head hung down against his soiled sombrero, barely touching the wooden porch floor. He was sobbing and snarling, blood gushing from his lips. Longarm aimed his rifle down over the man's chest and drilled one more merciful shot through the man's broad, tan forehead on which a bumblebee had been tattooed.

Longarm frowned down at the man, bringing his rifle back up.

Bumblebee Dan Halleran.

Longarm had once arrested Bumblebee Dan for robbing mail from the Butterfield line down in Arizona Territory. He'd heard the blond curly wolf, an Irish knife fighter and pistoleer, had escaped from the Yuma pen so long ago now that Longarm had since forgotten about him.

Well, here he was. Deader than hell. Right where he belonged. Longarm would have bet his right nut that it had been Bumblebee Dan who'd cut Dieter's head off and staked it along the trail to warn away a posse.

A gun hammer clicked behind Longarm, making the flesh on the back of his neck crawl.

Lowering the Winchester, he spun on his heel.

Chapter 12

"Jesus H. Christ! Put that fuckin' rifle down, ya son of a bitch! What are ya tryin' to do—kill *me, too?*"

There were a couple of planks stretched across two beer barrels at the back of the room, with burlap draped over the boards, and the old man poked his head out from under the planks as Longarm lifted the burlap with the barrel of his cocked Winchester.

What he'd thought was a gun being cocked was likely one of the old man's spurs scraping the floor as he cowered beneath the bar.

"Come on out of there, old-timer," Longarm ordered, backing away but keeping his rifle aimed from his hip. "And let me see those hands. If you have a pistol, you better drop it like a hot potato or I'll turn you out with your friends!"

"Friends?" the old man piped, huffing and wheezing as he crawled out from beneath the bar, the burlap catching on the back of his torn wool coat, which had been fashionable about twenty-five years ago. "They ain't no friends of mine. Hell, I figured they was friends of *yours!*"

He looked up at Longarm—a broad-faced, gray-bearded old man with thin gray hair that hung in two hide-wrapped pigtails down behind his shoulders. His floppy-brimmed black hat hung down his back from a horsehair thong.

"I don't shoot my *friends*," Longarm grouched.

The old man smiled cunningly, his lips thick and chapped in the tangled mass of his beard. "'Less there's a double cross on, eh? Oh, not that I give a rat's ass! I just came back fer some hooch!"

"Huh?"

"I work here. Leastways, I did—till the Indian agent up to Lone Pine put the Utes on the prod with some bad beef. They say that agent was sellin' some o' their squaws over to Denver as whores to boot."

The old man shook his head. "That'll do it every time. If it ain't the army piss-burnin' those red devils, it's the federal agents. Sure, I worked here till the stage line went outta business about a month ago. The wranglers and the Injun girl who cooked for me lit out for the hills, and I did, too—lookin' for the mother lode mostly. I keep my hooch here, though. In my cellar."

He grinned broadly, showing his tobacco-edged teeth and the several gaps where some had gone missing long ago. "Safe and *cool*! I'll share a little if you'll be so kind as to take that Winchester outta my face."

Longarm depressed the rifle's hammer and raised the barrel, planting the stock on his hip. Now that the dustup was over, he could feel the bullet burn across the outside of his right thigh. It felt as though a blacksmith had brushed it with a glowing andiron.

"Who're those two?" he asked, glancing at the man whose skull he'd crushed upon entering.

"Fang-toothed demons straight outta the devil's oven. Musta broke the doors o' Hell down and come a-runnin' back to kill and mangle."

The old man shuffled over to a table where an uncorked bottle sat surrounded by three shot glasses. A shabby green bowler sat near one of the glasses—probably the hat of the gent lying just inside the open back door. A playing card— a jack of spades—angled up from the hat's frayed silk band.

"They come about an hour ago," the old man continued. "Took me by surprise. I was down in my cellar, lookin' over my cache. I got it covered up again by the time they come into the lodge, so I only had to share one bottle with the sonso'bitches. I tell you 'cause you look like the honest sort, and I fancy myself a good judge o' character."

He held up the bottle. "Come on over and I'll pour ya a drink."

Longarm turned away from the oldster and sauntered over to the man he'd beaned with his rifle butt. The man stared up at Longarm, a grim, dead smile on his thin lips, chin sort of angled down and to one side. Sandy hair was sweat-pasted to his sunburned forehead, which was bloody and swollen where it had met up with the Winchester's brass butt plate.

Longarm's shaggy brows furrowed with befuddlement. The old man was staring at him, still holding the bottle in one hand, a glass in the other. "You're a lawman, ain't ya?"

Longarm didn't turn to him, but kept his curious gaze on the dead man. "How'd you know?"

"'Cause you ain't one o' them, but you got plenty of interest in 'em. I figured you for either a lawman or a bounty hunter. Bounty killers don't usually deck themselves out in ties and gold watch chains, though."

There was the splash of liquor into a glass, then the soft ticks of droplets running down the side of the glass and hitting the hard-packed earthen floor. "Trackin' 'em, are ya?"

The old man threw back the shot as Longarm nodded.

Likely, these two had been with the other two killed by the Utes, and somehow this pair had slipped away. The man on the floor had been saying as much before he'd opened the door and gotten his brains scrambled for his trouble. They were part of the group that had robbed the Silverjack wagon, killed Richard, and ambushed Dieter's men.

"Well, your job is done, Sheriff or Marshal or whoever the fuck ya is," said the old man, a little annoyance sounding in his voice. "Come on over and have a drink with me. I ain't drank with no one in a coon's age. Gets lonesome out here, don't ya know. The Injun girl who worked here used to share a bottle with me of a night out to the barn."

He chuckled. "Even gave me a little feel now and then. Big tits for such a silent, little thing."

"This ain't all of 'em," Longarm said with a sigh as he moseyed over to the table.

The old man had sat down. Looking eagerly up at Longarm, he tossed the whiskey out of one of the outlaw's glasses, and splashed in fresh.

"There was twelve total," Longarm said. "I've accounted for six. I wonder why they've been holding back."

He was speaking as much to himself as to the old man as he took the glass and stared down at the brown liquid with amber bubbles around the edges. "They had a good head start. They should be only a day away from Cimarron by now."

"I overheard 'em talkin' while I was fetchin' firewood," the old man said, sniffing his whiskey the way a gardener sniffs roses, a happy glow radiating from his rheumy hazel eyes. "I sorta gathered there was a double cross goin' down."

"Figures." Longarm sipped the whiskey. Not bad. The old man had gone easy on the gunpowder. He threw the rest back and absently enjoyed the swathing, edge-filing burn. "But where's the rest of 'em, and who has the loot?"

"Beats me," said the old man, reaching up and clinking the bottle's neck against the rim of Longarm's glass as he refilled it. "Maybe one of 'em buried it and they was supposed to go back later as a group for it. But these two got greedy."

"Maybe."

Longarm had crossed to the front of the lodge and stared down at the bloody, tattooed face of Bumblebee Dan, the lawman's eyes cast in deep thought. "If it's out here somewhere, that means the others will be back for it. So I might as well take my time getting to Cimarron."

It made sense, he figured. These two and the two killed by the Utes were holding back for a reason, and there could be no better reason than the stolen loot. The old man said they'd spoken of a double cross . . .

A grim smile twisted Longarm's lips. He might not have to run the others down after all. They might just come to him. Or come near enough to make his job . . . his purpose out here . . . a whole lot easier anyway.

"You got paper on them?" the old man said.

Longarm turned away from Bumblebee Dan and threw

back the rest of his hooch. "Nope. I ain't even out here official. I'm federal, and this is a local jurisdiction. They killed a friend of mine."

"So you're just makin' sure justice is done."

"Somethin' like that."

The old man chuckled knowingly as he threw back his whiskey, slammed the glass down drunkenly, and splashed more from the bottle. "You're on the gun trail then, ain't ya? Ain't no justice about it."

Longarm looked at him, feeling a nettled prick across the backs of his shoulders. "I'll give 'em a chance to give up."

"No, you won't." The old man laughed, wheezing, turning his head slightly to narrow an eye at Longarm. "And why the hell should you? Like you said, you ain't out here official-like, right?"

The old man lifted his glass in salute and threw back the whiskey. Angry without realizing why, Longarm set his glass on a nearby table and opened the lodge's front door. As he stepped out to take a look around, a clatter rose in the distance. It was the wagon, the mules coming on slowly, the girls sitting in the driver's box with a stiff, tentative air.

Shit, he'd forgotten about the Lyndecker girls.

He leaned his rifle against the lodge's front wall near the open door, then went back inside. Ignoring the burn in his thigh, he dragged the dead man near the back door into the backyard, behind the two-hole privy sheathed in lilac bushes and sage.

Heading back inside the lodge, in which the old man continued drinking at his table, a dreamy expression in his eyes as he stared out the open window right of the door at the wagon pulling up to the stock tank, Longarm gave

Bumblebee Dan's boots a brusque shove over the window ledge.

Then he went out, hooked Dan's feet under his arm, and mimicking a draft animal, began pulling the man's limp, bloody carcass off the porch and into the yard.

"Jesus!" Randi exclaimed, making a face as she wrapped the wagon's ribbons around the brake handle.

Birt grinned down at Longarm, raking her blue-eyed gaze between the lawman and the dead man carving a furrow in the dirt and dried manure behind him. "Turn another one toe-down, Longarm? Buck him out in a hail of *hot lead*?"

The girl lurched forward on her seat, lifting her shoulders and pressing her hands down between her thighs in orgasmic glory.

"Somethin' like that," Longarm growled, dragging Bumblebee Dan past the wagon toward the old springhouse, where he intended to leave the notorious jasper for the wolves and coyotes. "We'll stay here for the night. Why don't you two unhitch the mules and the roan, and lead 'em into the barn yonder? I'll be along shortly."

When Longarm had deposited Bumblebee Dan behind the springhouse, he found the pinto out by the creek that twisted through the brushy hummocks just west of the lodge.

He took a good look around. Seeing no sign of more outlaws or Utes, he rummaged around in his saddlebags for his bottle of Maryland rye. He took the rye down to the creek and leaned it against a rock while he kicked off his boots, peeled off his socks, then shucked out of his summer underwear and whipcord trousers.

Naked from the waist down, he leaned back against a

rock and inspected the burn across the outside of his right thigh. Only about a quarter inch deep. Not serious, but it would nettle him for days and take its own sweet time healing.

He dabbed at the blood with a handkerchief, and cursed as he sucked air through his teeth. The blood had already congealed over the wound. Pushing himself up, he shucked out of his coat, tie, vest, and shirt, and stepped off the creek bank and into the deep pool of a beaver pond. The bracingly cool water rose up his thighs.

He stopped in the middle of the mud-bottomed pond, soaked the handkerchief, and set to work dabbing at the dried blood, chewing his lower lip as he worked. He glanced at the sky.

The sun was dropping in the west. Still several hours of daylight left, but the mule's hock needed tending. His own thigh could do with a rest as well.

Besides, it looked like the owlhoots were in no hurry getting to Cimarron. The other six might still be out here somewhere, looking for the loot two or three of the others had decided to make their own. The double-crossers might have decided to bury the box and wait for the fury over it to die down, then dig it up again, take it south through Arizona, and sell it across the border in Mexico.

The other thieves and killers probably got wind of it somehow—double crosses hardly ever worked the way the double-crossers intended—and were scurrying around out here, looking for it while trying to stay one step ahead of the piss-burned Utes.

"Need any help out there, Longarm?"

Birt's voice jerked the lawman's head up with a start. He staggered backward in the cool water, and nearly fell over a branch curving up from the pond's bottom.

Birt was sitting on the creek bank, near where he'd left his gun and his pants. The saddled pinto stood behind her, lowering his head to fondly sniff the girl's wheat-colored hair, which fell down around her shoulders in a thick, sunlit mass.

Chapter 13

Longarm covered his privates with both hands and stood there in the thigh-deep water, gritting his teeth with fury. "What the hell you think you're doing? I came over here for a little privacy, damnit!"

"Looks to me like you came to clean that bullet burn," Birt said. "Maybe I better come out there and help. A man needs a woman's soft touch every now and then. Even one as wild and woolly as the Long Arm of the Law his own-self!"

"You stay where you are," Longarm ordered, removing one hand from his crotch to thrust an arm toward the girl, one finger jutting like a pistol barrel.

He didn't like being caught with his pants down—literally or figuratively, even by as pretty a girl as Birt. It was embarrassing. When a girl saw him naked, he liked to be prepared, and he liked it to be his idea!

"What—you want me to just sit here and watch?" she asked.

Longarm flushed, annoyed and confused, unable to keep his eyes from darting down to the girl's low-cut summer frock, which revealed nearly half of her deep, creamy cleavage. As usual, she wasn't wearing underwear, and he could see the outline of each large, pear-shaped breast sloping down her chest and pointing slightly out to each side.

"No, damnit. I meant"—he jerked his arm wide—"get the hell out of here and let me tend my *own* damn bullet burn!"

Birt blinked, her even-featured, smooth-skinned face retaining an air of studied, coquettish mockery. "I've seen you staring at my titties, Longarm. There's only us out here. There ain't no Injuns or badmen. Hell, even Randi's set to work packin' the mule's hock. She's good at doctorin' mules—Randi. Me—I'm good at doctorin' men. Why, back home in Dakota, I healed a neighbor boy after he ran his horse through barbed wire in a rainstorm."

"That's right dandy. But this is just a . . ."

Longarm was trying to keep his mind focused and clear. Out here, danger was liable to raise its ugly head from behind any hogback. If not Utes, outlaws. But his mind abandoned him suddenly, and he heard his voice trail off as the girl reached down in front of her, grabbing her dress down low and pulling it up and over her head.

She tossed it into the brush near Longarm's strewn clothes and shell belt.

She sat creamy-naked before him, long, fine legs curled slightly beneath her. As she leaned back on an outstretched arm, her pale breasts—a good handful each—sloped out to the side, pink-nippled, ripe, and tender. For a stretched second, Longarm imagined turning one of the delicate, rose-petal nipples between his lips.

A burst of anger slammed the door on the thought, and he filled his lungs to order her once more away from here. But before he could do more than bunch his lips, she unfolded her naked legs and rose. Breasts jerking from side to side, her white teeth glistening between her spread, pink lips, she strode over to the water and dipped a toe.

"Cold!"

Admonishing words caught like a bone in Longarm's throat. His eyes raked her up and down and sideways, and when they were done, they started all over again. His pulse throbbed in his temples, and he felt a tightness in his chest—like he'd been hammered once by a heavy fist over his heart.

"You better talk nice to me, Lawdog," she said in a sexy-husky, chastising voice as, wincing a little and throwing her thin arms out for balance, she stepped into the beaver pond. "Or I won't be near as gentle as I could be."

"I . . . I told you to stay where you were," Longarm said, his voice sounding far away and hollow as he watched the girl move toward him in all her young, ripe beauty.

Her hair bounced slightly on her shoulders and buffeted out from her rosy cheeks in the breeze. Her breasts shifted from side to side. She had a few moles, Longarm vaguely noticed—one just above her left breast, one just below the right, and another about two inches above and to the left of her belly button. They were a shade darker than the skin around them, and they somehow ratcheted up her desirability by several inexplicable notches.

Her little snatch was the same color as her hair, and it glistened brightly as the water rose up and dampened it.

"You're getting a boner, Longarm," she said accusingly, her wide eyes on his crotch.

Longarm looked down. He held only one hand over his privates, and it did nothing to cover the erect, hard shaft of his purple-headed cock angling up over his belly button.

"I just came out to do some doctorin', and you're gettin'

your blood all up. You must like to fuck as much as you like to shoot and throw a loop over outlaws and drag 'em to justice."

She stood before him, a coy look on her delicately featured face, covering one breast with her arm while cupping pond water over the other one. "Ain't that right?"

Longarm no longer felt stupid and foolish for letting himself get caught out here in his birthday suit. His pulse had worked up a thunderstorm in his head, and his blood boiled in his veins. He found himself reaching forward and grabbing the girl's arms in his hands, trying in his sudden carnal haste not to squeeze too hard.

"Your sister told me you were pure," he said, narrowing an eye at the wanton blond filly, a wing of his hair flopping down over his forehead as a late-afternoon breeze picked up.

Birt laughed. "She tells folks that, but Randi's the pure one. I don't think she's ever been with a man. At least"— her eyes dropped to Longarm's dong lifting its big head above the tea brown water—"not a *real* man. She told you that 'cause she wants you for herself."

She reached out and wrapped one hand around his shaft, gently squeezing, her lusty grin broadening. Electric shock waves nipped at Longarm's loins, and he steadied his feet on the bottom of the pond.

"Oh, she never told me in so many words," said Birt. "Randi don't like to talk about such things. It makes her bashful."

Birt crouched down, glanced up at Longarm, then holding his cock in her right fist, planted a delicate kiss on its swollen head.

He swallowed.

Pulling her head back and keeping her face turned toward his member, as though speaking to his dong, she said, "As you can see, I'm not bashful at all."

She swallowed. Gooseflesh lay across her breasts and shoulders. Her nipples jutted slightly out to either side. She glanced up at him, a sudden, hard, desperate yearning in her eyes.

"In fact, if you don't use this thing on me soon, I'm just gonna die, Lawdog!"

Longarm looked around quickly, making sure they were still alone. Then he pulled her head and shoulders up above the water, and crouched as he snaked one hand under her knees, the other under her neck. She gave a little, surprised scream as, with a hungry, passionate grunt, he swept her up out of the splashing water and cradled her across his chest, pond water streaming down her legs and feet and toes as he carried her back toward shore.

She clung to his neck, and he could hear her heart beating in her chest, feel the rush of her blood in her veins. As he stepped up out of the creek and strode toward their strewn clothes, the pinto eyeing them suspiciously, she nuzzled his neck, planting soft but hungry kisses under his ear.

"Fuck me," she moaned, sounding like a half-feral cat. "Fuck me, Longarm. Fuck me. Fuck me . . ."

His face a mask of grim purpose, his chest rising and falling slowly, heavily, the muscles in his arms bulging, he laid her down atop their clothes. He leaned forward, and she spread her legs for him, hooking her wrists under her knees and opening herself even wider as she drew her legs back toward her ears. He crouched over her, sliding his heavy, throbbing rod into position. She grunted and groaned, desperately holding her legs as far apart as possible without splitting herself in two.

Her breasts spilled across her chest, heaping scoops of

cream, nipples jutting. She sucked a sharp breath between
gritted teeth, and he did the same as she set her heels atop
his back and ground her fingers into his buttocks, pulling
him into her and lifting her chin so high, tipping her head
back, that the cords in her neck stood out.

He fucked her for several minutes slowly, sliding in and
out with a deft rhythm, her curled legs and pink feet bouncing up high at his sides like hairless pink wings. She moaned
and sighed, shuddering and grinding her fingers into his ass.

When he could feel her snatch spasming around his pistoning shaft, he rose up onto his arms and his toes, breathing hard, his face turning brick red from lust and exertion,
and hammered her home.

When Longarm and Birt had caught their breath, lounging
atop their mingled clothes, he tossed her his neckerchief
and pointed to the bloody burn across the outside of his
thigh. With a soft, supplicant grunt, she kissed his spent
cock lying like a dead fish against his leg, took the handkerchief, and ran over to the pond to soak it.

When she returned, she lay down beside him and slowly,
carefully cleaned the wound with a corner of the damp
cloth. Neither one said anything. Longarm lay back against
a hooked arm, watching her work.

She looked up at him occasionally with an oblique half
smile. Then she'd lean down, nuzzle his cock and balls, and
continue dabbing the damp cloth at the burn with matronly
attention.

Longarm half dozed as the girl worked on him. He was
thoroughly enjoying their sojourn down here by the beaver
pond. Damn apt name for the water, he thought with a fur-
tive grin.

He remembered his frolic with Cynthia in the mountains

above Grand View without chagrin. They'd agreed to nothing except to have the best time possible when they were together, and to honor each other's freedom when they were apart.

That day above Grand View seemed long ago now, but it had only been—what? Two, maybe three days. He'd lost track. She and the general and Mrs. Larimer were no doubt back in Denver, Cynthia likely packing to head off once more for some country or city Longarm had never heard of, let alone visited.

He remembered her painting, and again he grinned.

"What's funny?" Birt asked, smiling down at him.

"Nothing."

She nudged him with her elbow. "Tell me."

"If you have to know, I was remembering another time like this."

"With another girl?"

"Couldn't have been you, could it—since this was our first time?"

She turned the corners of her mouth down as she lay naked beside him, creamy and ripe, blond hair spilling over a shoulder and across a breast. Her hand with the cloth in it rested on his leg.

"You been with a lot of women, Lawdog?"

"My share," he grunted.

"This ain't gonna be our one and only time, is it?"

"Sometimes once is enough," he said, closing one eye at her. "If it was good enough."

He rose up on his elbows and looked down at the burn. "Not bad."

"Will be there anything else?" The coy, sensuous smile returned as she leaned down slowly to rest her cheek against his cock.

He felt the pull again in his loins. His member responded, stirring like a snake. She felt it, and rose up onto her hands and knees. Looking back over her shoulder at him, she spread her legs, wagged her bottom, and grimaced with want.

"Oh, hell," he said, looking around.

He climbed onto his hands and knees and, never one to turn down doggie style, placed his hands on her hips and took the shuddering girl from behind.

They'd no sooner finished, Birt groaning facedown in the grass, than a scream rose from the direction of the lodge.

Longarm jerked his head up.

"Randi!" Birt cried, reaching for her dress.

Chapter 14

Longarm scrambled into his pants, boots, and hat, and grabbing his shell belt, hightailed it toward the cabin. He leaped rocks and sage shrubs as he awkwardly buckled the belt around his waist, and sprinted into the station yard just as a rifle cracked inside the lodge.

"Varmint!" Randi's voice shouted.

"Please! *No!*" a man cried.

KA-BLAM!

Longarm had his .44 in his hand as he leaped up the three porch steps in a single bound.

The rifle boomed again, echoing around the lodge's adobe brick walls as Longarm bulled through the open timber door and instinctively stepped to one side, so he wouldn't be backlit by the entrance.

"I apologize!" the old, gray-bearded man cried again as he bolted out from behind one table near the lodge's far right wall and dove behind another, turning it over so that it toppled down in front of him.

He glanced out from behind it, his eyes bright with terror. "I won't do it again, young lady—I *promise*!" His eyes slid toward Longarm. "Mister, please . . . *stop* her!"

"Stop *this*, you horny old bastard!" Randi shouted as she ejected a spent cartridge from a Spencer carbine she must have found somewhere in the lodge.

Standing near the table at which the old man had been sitting when Longarm had last seen him, she raised the carbine to her shoulder. Longarm strode forward. The old man yowled and drew his head back behind the table he used as a shield as Randi triggered the old rifle once more.

The slug hammered the table's scarred surface six inches to the right of where the old man's head had been, chewing a ragged hole.

"Damnit!" the old man bellowed. "That damn near took my ear off!"

"Next one's gonna take your old pecker off!" Randi shouted.

Longarm grabbed the Spencer just after she'd jerked down the trigger guard cocking lever, sending the smoking shell casing dancing around the dirt floor at her bare feet. In her rage and with the gunfire, she hadn't heard him coming, and she gave an angry, snarling scream as he jerked the rifle from her hands.

"That's enough, girl!" Longarm said. "What the hell're you trying to do—*kill* him?"

"You're damn right I am!" she snapped, her enraged brown eyes dropping from the lawman's face to rake across his broad, chestnut-furred chest clad in only his suspender straps. Her eyes softened slightly and her mouth opened, but she seemed to have trouble finding the words.

Finally, she flung her arm out toward the old man's shielding table. "He . . . he grabbed my tit!"

"That right, mister?" Longarm called to the table.

The old man edged one rheumy, fear-bright eye out from behind the table. Then the other.

Seeing that Longarm had disarmed the girl, he gave a sigh and said with a schoolboy's chagrin, "Ah, hell, I was helpin' her unload her damn wagon, and . . . and . . . well, hell, I ain't had no purty girl around for a coon's age . . ."

His eyes shifted to the door behind Longarm as Birt ran into the lodge, her cheeks flushed with worry. "Damn!" the old man said. "You mean there's *two* of 'em? One smoky-eyed and dark, and the other"—his eyes sparked with lascivious interest and his voice thickened—"creamy-skinned . . . and fair."

Randi grabbed for the Spencer in Longarm's hands. "Give me that, damn ya, Longarm! I'm gonna perforate that old—!"

"Randi!" Birt yelled as Longarm held the rifle high above the brunette's head with one hand and held her back with the other. "For chrissakes, he's just an old man. Leave him be." The blonde splayed her hand on her opulent bosom through her thin dress. "I thought it was *you* gettin' shot in here! Damn near gave me a heart stroke!"

Randi gave up on the rifle. She frowned suspiciously at her sister. "Where the hell've you been?" She cut her eyes at Longarm, dropped her gaze again to his bare chest. "Where the hell've you *both* been?"

"I was . . ." Birt glanced off guiltily and rolled a strand of her blond hair on her finger. ". . . takin' a walk . . ."

"What about you?" Randi asked Longarm.

The lawman was ejecting the last three shells from the Spencer's breech. "None of your damn business! Now, why don't you leave the old man and your sis alone, and quit informing every Ute in the territory where we are! Then you can both make yourselves useful by starting supper!"

With that, he tossed the rifle at the old-timer, who caught it against his chest, and then the lawman stomped on out of the roadhouse.

"I packed the mule's leg for ya," Randi jeered behind him.

"It ain't my mule!" Longarm shouted back without turning around. "And if you shoot that old reprobate while I fetch my clothes from the creek, I'll hang ya from the nearest tree!"

He kicked a stone. Birt had been one fine, stress-relieving tussle on the bank of the beaver pond. But here he was—sick to the gills of both Lyndecker girls once again.

"Damn," said the old man, whose name Longarm had learned was Hank Maclean. "Those two little pieces of ass sure can cook!"

He wheezed a laugh and puffed his corncob pipe as he and Longarm, sitting in wicker chairs on the roadhouse's front porch, watched the last light bleed from the western sky, darkening the ragged peaks before them.

Longarm puffed a nickel cheroot and scratched his thumbnail at a lump of mud and horse dung stuck to the heel of his right cavalry boot. He was feeling refreshed and satisfied after his and Birt's rutting by the pond and the good meal of antelope stew and wild greens she and Randi had thrown together.

"I'd keep my voice down if I was you," he warned Maclean. "'Less you want sweet little Randi to take your Spencer from you again and poke it up your ass, which I wouldn't put past her."

The girls were conversing inside, their shadows jostling in the light pushing out from the lodge's open door. Pots

and pans clattered, wash water splashed, and there was the
scrape of steel wool on cast iron.

Maclean shook his head. "Jesus, what a damned embarrassing thing. A purty little girl like that chasin' me around
with my own rifle. If my dear old dead partners seen that,
they're still spinning in their graves for sure. Likely so
dizzy, they're pukin'!"

He removed the pipe from his mouth and squinted an
eye at Longarm. "I learned one thing from that little experience, though."

"What's that?"

Maclean lowered his voice and leaned his head closer to
Longarm's shoulder. "Girl's got a nice handful under that
man's work shirt o' hers!"

The oldster wheezed another laugh, thoroughly pleased
with himself.

"Say," he said when he'd caught his breath, "what were
you and the little blonde doin' down by the creek?"

"She was tending my bullet wound."

"Really?"

Longarm puffed his cheroot and stared off, the back of
his neck feeling as though the afternoon sun were on it.
"Really."

"Pshaw . . ." the old man said uncertainly.

"Never mind them girls, old-timer," Longarm growled.
"How far is it from here to Cimarron?"

Maclean repositioned himself in his chair, making the
wicker squawk and puffing his pipe. He loosed a rancid-
smelling fart and said, "A long day from here. With a
wagon, you're probably looking at a day and a half. Think
it's about forty miles, but the last twenty are through
rough, hilly country." He glanced at Longarm through a

gray black fog of pipe smoke, narrowing a shaded eye. "And if them owlhoots are threading them hills, lookin' for the loot . . ."

"I know," Longarm said with a sigh, rolling his cheroot from one side of his mouth to the other. "We'll have to dodge 'em. It ain't like I can track 'em when I got the girls to worry about."

He was speaking to himself again as much as to Maclean. "I'll have to pull straight through to Cimarron, get shed of the girls and the wagon. Then I'll get some fresh saddle horses and backtrack, clean up as many of that scum as I can find."

Longarm gritted his teeth as his dying friend, Richard Collins, floated up in his mind, as did the hacked-off head of Sheriff Dieter. His gun hand twitched.

"Now you're talkin' like a bounty killer," Maclean said, glancing at Longarm's right hand, the fingers of which the lawman was pressing into his thigh. "And I don't blame ya one damn bit."

Longarm felt that inexplicable annoyance again. It was a burn at the base of his spine. And he didn't like it.

Why the hell shouldn't he hunt down the killers of Richard Collins and kill each one just like they'd killed Richard—without mercy? He wasn't a lawman now. Officially, he was still on vacation. Officially, he was still poking Cynthia Larimer in the hills above Grand View.

Now he was the friend of a murdered man. Now he was on the gun trail, looking to avenge his friend.

The problem was, he realized suddenly as he stared at the last rosy glow dimming between dark, ragged peaks, he kept seeing the image of his boss, Billy Vail, in his head as well. It came right on the tail of Richard's image.

And he knew what Billy would tell him to do.

No. Not tell him. He knew what Billy would *expect* him to do.

"Ah, fuck it!" he groused, rising from his chair and flicking his cheroot butt into the yard beyond the porch.

"What's that?" Maclean said, looking up at him, surprised and wary.

"I'm gonna sleep out under the stars," Longarm said, grabbing his Winchester from against the cabin wall. "You stay inside with the girls. But leave 'em alone, hear?"

As Longarm tramped out into the night, his rifle on his shoulder, he heard Maclean say, softly chuckling, behind him, "I reckon they'll see to that!"

Longarm had a fitful night's rest as he kept watch for more Utes and for the killers on the scout for the strongbox. He made sure the place remained dark all night, but the searching gang members would no doubt be attracted to the lodge like bugs to lantern light.

After a quick breakfast at false dawn, he and the girls got an early start, even Randi bidding good-bye to Hank Maclean as the oldster smoked his pipe, hummed "Oh! Susanna," and led his mule by a frayed rope into the low hills east of the roadhouse.

Mid-morning, Longarm left the stage road and took a shortcut that Maclean had told him about last night before turning in. It was an old freight trail the cavalry had once used, but abandoned after the Utes had burned a fort just west of Cimarron.

A fork in the trail still led to Cimarron, however, though the old man warned that it might be faint. And the fork might be hard to find, though it lay just beyond a cottonwood copse in a narrow, rock-walled canyon known as the Mad Woman Fork of the Cimarron River.

The shortcut followed a meandering dry wash through the sage and yellow and red wildflowers, rock escarpments pushing up on both sides, above the wash's alkali, stone-strewn bottom. Just past noon and riding about thirty yards ahead of the wagon, Longarm looked around, squinting at the bright sky slowly filling with ragged, purple-edged clouds.

He'd seen no Indian sign all morning, and though he'd scouted the country several times, he'd spied no riders on his and the girls' backtrail. In the open stretches of prairie showing between bluffs on both sides of the wash, he'd seen no telltale dust plumes or sun flashes off tack or hardware.

Still, the skin was stretched taut between his shoulder blades. His shoulders themselves were tight and heavy, as though mortared into their sockets.

He knew that feeling too well. It was the feeling that told him something was wrong. Exactly *what* was wrong, he didn't know.

It could mean they were indeed being followed. Or it might mean they were riding into an ambush. Or, hell, maybe the girls in the wagon weren't human, but some alien creatures dropped out of the sky to bedevil him for all his past sins.

In other words, he had no idea why he felt the way he did. But he knew from past experience that his shoulders didn't lie. They usually knew before his brain did that he was riding into trouble.

And he seldom knew from which direction it would come until it came.

Trouble came sooner than expected a few minutes later, in the form of cold raindrops blowing against his back, instantly chilling him. Thunder rumbled. He glanced over his shoulder to see his horse's tail blowing straight up in the air and a witch's finger of lightning flashing just above and behind the wagon.

Amidst the flash, a gray curtain of rain barreled toward him. His heart thumped as he glanced around the shallow, sandy wash.

If those clouds were as pregnant as they looked, the arroyo would be a raging river in minutes. And unless the Lyndecker girls were indeed aliens—aliens with flippers and gills—they'd be rolled asunder and drowned!

Chapter 15

Longarm ducked his head and tipped his hat against the wind as he reined the roan around and rode back to the wagon.

"Whip up those mules and get 'em moving!" he shouted to the girls sitting in the driver's boot, their hair flying as the wind swirled and thunder rumbled. "I'm gonna ride ahead and look for cover!"

He paused as a thunderclap hammered, making the ground shake and causing the roan to fiddle-foot and the mules to bray.

Holding the horse's reins taut, he yelled, "If this wash starts to fill, head for the grass on either side!"

"Okay!" Birt cried, shaking the ribbons over the mules' backs.

As the mules leaned into their collars, Longarm booted the roan on up the wash. Horse and rider galloped around a bend and, a hundred yards beyond it, Longarm spied a copse of wind- and rain-tossed cottonwoods up a rise low enough for the mules to climb. There were a couple of rocky outcrops amongst the trees, and these and the cottonwoods would offer cover for him and the girls as well as the stock.

He reined the roan back toward the wagon.

The mules had stopped. They stood in their collars and hames, shaking their heads with characteristic stubbornness. The rain hammered like billions of white javelins.

The heavens popped and roared. Lightning flashed wickedly just over and around the wagon, close enough that Longarm could smell the brimstone.

The girls leaned forward from the driver's seat, their bare feet propped on the dashboard. Their mouths opened and closed, but Longarm couldn't hear their yells above the wind, thunder, and rain. The mules likely couldn't either. He couldn't even hear the wet, sucking clomps of the roan's hooves in the quickly filling wash.

Cursing to himself, he leaped down from the roan's back, ran over to the mules, grabbed the left one's collar, and pulled. No good. It wouldn't budge. Meanwhile, the wash had become a stream, and foaming clay-colored water was rising to the animals' hocks.

"You stubbornnest-assed sonso'bitches!" Longarm yelled, ramming a wet-gloved fist against the right mule's collar. It made a wet thump, spraying water.

He looked around wildly. Up the wash's left bank was a copse of scattered pine and aspens. Above the trees lay a sandstone dike that rose up and out over the slope from its base, offering a roof of sorts. It was a good hundred yards away, and a stiff climb, but he and the girls had no choice.

He slopped through the rising water to the front of the wagon. The rain sluiced off his hat—enough to fill a rain barrel in fifteen minutes. It dribbled down his back and weighed down his clothes, making his boots feel like lead weights on his feet. When he was near the wagon's left front wheel, he looked up at the two soaked girls, who regarded him desperately, their hair pasted to their faces.

"Grab what you need and hightail it up there!" Longarm shouted, jerking his thumb toward the dike.

"Up *where*?" Randi asked.

"Those rocks yonder!" Longarm started unhitching the team.

"What about the mules?" Birt yelled.

"I'm gonna turn 'em loose! They'll stick around!"

"What about the *wagon*?" Randi wanted to know.

"It'll be all right here till the flood dies down." Longarm gave both girls sharp, impatient looks as he hurried to free the double-tree. "Haul your asses, goddamnit! That lightning's coming closer, and this ain't no little spring daisy-dappler!"

"We can't leave the wagon!" both girls shouted at nearly the same time, their soaked faces bunched with worry and pleading.

Longarm was exasperated as he sloshed through the mud to remove the tack from the mules' backs. He twisted around, fighting to keep his footing as the floodwaters rose to nearly his knees. "No one's gonna steal your goddamn freight! Now, do like I said or I'll take you both over my knee and tan your bare bottoms!"

The girls looked at each other. Then Randi reluctantly climbed over the back of the driver's box and ducked through the wagon's front pucker. Birt followed. The girls slipped out of the wagon a minute later, both hefting or dragging burlap sacks, war bags, and bedrolls.

Having freed the mules from the wagon, Longarm had started leading the roan and the pinto up the slope through the pines and aspens. The horses whinnied and fiddle-footed more vigorously with every lightning flash and thunderclap.

"Come on!" he shouted, beckoning angrily to the girls, his voice nearly drowned by another nearby thunderclap that sounded like boulder-sized cymbals smashed together by God.

Both Lyndecker girls stood on the shore of the churning wash, casting frustrated glances at the wagon and at each other before turning and slogging barefoot up the slope behind Longarm.

They crouched beneath their heavy, unwieldy burdens and the slanting, hammering rain. The mules, free of the wagon, brayed as they climbed the bank and headed, buck-kicking, into the shelter of the wind-pummeled trees, whipping their tails.

Longarm stopped long enough for the girls to catch up to him, and looped a couple of their bags over the roan's saddle. "Jesus, what is all this stuff? We're not stayin' for a month!"

But his shouts were drowned by the storm. As the girls continued slogging up the hill, both barefoot but seemingly oblivious to the pine needles and cones, Longarm jerked the frightened horses onward, meandering around the narrow posts of the trees.

When they were halfway up the slope, there was a sudden blue white flash off to Longarm's right. It seemed to suck the breath from his lungs. Then, as he heard the sizzle and the popping sounds of a falling tree, a thunderclap roared, shaking the ground beneath his feet.

The girls screamed and pranced sideways, dropping their bags to cover their ears. The horses whinnied, and the roan nearly broke loose of Longarm's grip, pulling the lawman down on one knee before he reaffirmed his hold.

"Fuck!" Longarm bellowed at the gods who'd loosed the storm on him, on top of everything else. *"Fuck you cocksuckin' sonso'bitches!"*

"Who're you yelling at?" Randi cried, rain sluicing down her head and cheeks and nose.

Her wet, dark brown hair hung straight down to her shoulders. Her men's clothes were stuck so tightly against her that it wasn't hard at all to see that she was quite the curvaceous young woman—at least from the hips up.

The vision of her and her sister standing there, soaked to the gills, perked Longarm's primitive male spirits up and, grumbling, he gained his feet once more and urged the horses on up the hill as the fallen lightning-struck pine sparked and sizzled up the hill to his right. It filled the rain-fresh air with the smell of scorched pine sap and brimstone.

He and the girls made the escarpment ten minutes later. It was even better cover than Longarm had thought, for there was a long, deep gap along the bottom, with the top of the dike arching a good thirty feet over the slope.

It formed a long, shallow cave. There even appeared a stone fire ring left by previous travelers.

"Go on up!" Longarm shouted to the girls, who slipped and fell on the muddy slope above the trees. "I'll be along after I picket the horses!"

The rain hammered him, gushing off his hat brim and onto his chest and shoulders, as he strung a picket line between two pines, then unsaddled the roan. Leaving the mounts as protected as possible, he hauled his tack up the muddy slope toward the cave.

He thought he smelled smoke, but it had to be that fallen pine still smoldering after the lightning strike.

Just under the dike's overhang, he stopped and stared down with surprise at the stone ring in which a fire danced, sizzling when raindrops blew in from outside. Pine boughs lay on one side of the fire. Birt's dress was spread across half of the boughs while Randi's flannel shirt, denims, and cotton underwear occupied the other half.

Both girls sat on the fire's backside, knees drawn up to their chests, bare toes protruding from the gray wool army blankets wrapped snug around their bodies. They sat hunched against the cold wind, as close to the fire as possible, their hair plastered to their heads.

They both looked owly and miserable.

Birt tossed her head to indicate behind her, and said glumly and just loudly enough to be heard above the storm's din, "Someone left dry firewood. We had matches in our possible bags. Come and get warm, Lawdog. You look like you just swam the seven seas."

Longarm glanced at the pile of wood stacked against an inside wall of the cave. It was a common custom to leave wood and sometimes even food in far-flung outback shelters, and Longarm was glad the custom had been adhered to here.

He dropped his gear just inside the cave, shucked his rifle from its boot, and dropped down beside the fire. He tossed his hat onto the pine boughs and rested his rifle across his thighs, running his hands straight back through his wet hair.

"You best get outta them clothes, Lawdog," Birt said, planting her chin on her upraised knees and smiling ever so slightly. "You'll catch your death o' cold in them wet duds."

Randi shot her sister a snide look. "You'd just like that, wouldn't you?"

"A dead man can't take us to Cimarron, Miss Prissy Sis!"

"You're just a damn bitch in heat—that's what you are!" Randi retorted, lifting her head and dropping her blanket low enough to reveal the first beguiling rise of her tan cleavage. "Ma and Pa named us crossways. You're the one that shoulda been named *Randi*!"

"Ain't nothin' *randy* about keepin' the man alive, is there?"

"You just wanna see his dong!"

"No, I don't!"

Now their faces were about two inches apart and their fists were clenched, blankets tumbling off their shoulders, as Randi shrilled, "Do, too! And don't try to tell me you ain't already seen it neither, 'cause—!"

"All right, all right!" Longarm interjected, rolling his eyes. "Neither one of you damn she-cats is gonna see my dong. I'm keepin' my pants and everything else on. I've been wet before, and I'll be wet again, and I'll dry just fine here by the fire."

He hardened his jaws, and his steely eyes spat sparks. "Now, both of you shut the fuck up or I'm gonna take you down to the wash and hold your heads under till the rest of you is all done *twitchin'*!"

"You just try it!" both girls warned at the same time, their own eyes flashing flames.

They stared at Longarm like two panthers ready to pounce. Longarm stared back at them like a rogue grizzly ready to rip and tear. Between the girls and the storm—not to mention the owlhoots and the Indians—he was ready to explode.

Randi's eyes were the first to soften and drop to the fire. A second later, Birt's gaze retreated from Longarm's, and she pulled her blanket up high across her shoulders and jaws, and drew her knees closer to her chest.

Hunkering low, like a rabbit in its hole, she clamped one bare foot over the other, and neither girl said anything for a long, long time—not while Longarm found a dry cheroot amongst his gear and took his time smoking it, watching the storm.

Not while he built up the fire and threw his frock and vest over a rock to dry.

Not while he made coffee and then got out his cook pots and pans and rustled up a supper of bacon and pinto beans.

Only when the food was done and he'd shoveled grub onto three plates and shoved two in front of the sulking girls, did Birt turn up her nose and say, "I ain't hungry."

"Eat it. You're gonna need it. Storm or no storm, tomorrow we're pushing on to Cimarron."

Long after both girls had rolled up in their blankets near the fire, Longarm had one last smoke and stared into the stormy darkness. The brunt of the storm had passed, but a chill mist continued. The pines dripped.

Otherwise, the night was as silent as the bottom of a well.

He might as well turn in, too. No Utes or outlaws would be stalking around on a night like this.

His clothes were nowhere near dry. He glanced at Birt and Randi curled up in their blankets, hair fanned out beneath their heads, the fire's red flames shunting shadows across their faces. Both girls snored softly.

Longarm stood and shucked out of his pants and underwear, and tossed them with the girls' duds on the pine boughs. He tossed two more hefty logs onto the fire, then got down and rolled up in his blankets.

He was asleep before his head hit the saddle.

Something touched his shoulder. He jerked his head up and closed his hand around the walnut grips of his .44.

Something held it fast to its holster. A pink, mud-streaked foot was clamped over the gun and the holster, the toes grinding into the leather.

He looked up.

Randi stood over him, a blanket wrapped around her shoulders. Her dry hair hung straight down, obscuring her face.

"That ain't the rod you need, Lawdog."

She dropped the blanket.

She'd been wearing nothing under it.

Chapter 16

Fleeing Longarm's snores and the cave's hard stone floor, Birt had gone down to sleep on the soft dry goods sacks in the wagon.

Now Longarm hammered away between her sister's spread legs. Randi lay back on her elbows, a look of fierce anguish crumpling her pretty features. She sobbed and groaned, her head bouncing, hair dancing, with each savage thrust of Longarm's powerful hips.

"Oh," Randi cried. "I never . . . knew it . . . like . . . this!" Her lower jaw dropped and her eyes snapped wide. *"Ahhhh!"*

Longarm dropped down to the girl's warm, damp chest. A still-firm nipple caressed his nose.

Randi threw her head back against the ground and laughed luxuriously, grinding her heels into Longarm's lower back. Her body spasmed beneath him.

"Glad ya enjoyed it," Longarm growled, still owly from having been awakened from a nice, deep sleep.

The girl's nipple moved as she breathed.

He smelled pipe smoke.

"Go ahead," Randi said.

Longarm lifted his head, frowning up at the girl's face.

She stared into the shadows behind him.

"Go ahead and do it!" she ordered.

Longarm glanced over his shoulder. He caught a fleeting glimpse of Birt's pale face and jostling blond hair before something hard smashed against his temple.

Javelins of burning pain plundering his skull, he collapsed against Randi's heaving breasts. As the darker Lyndecker girl scuttled out from beneath him, Longarm rolled over on his back, clutching at consciousness the way a falling man grabs for a rope.

"I'm sorry, Lawdog," he heard Birt say in a tremulous, distant voice.

His eyes fluttered, the lids growing heavy. He tried to rise, but his muscles were turning quickly to water and the cave floor pitched and rolled beneath him. Through a haze of bright pink pain, he looked up to see a bearded face smiling down at him. Hank Maclean poked his corncob pipe between his lips, puffing smoke, and then the oldster's face blurred away into darkness.

There was a long, miserable, nightmare-laden sleep, until Longarm finally opened his eyes to find himself cheek-down against the cave floor. His arms ached so badly that he'd dreamt that little men in peaked caps and goat beards were chuckling delightfully as they hammered rail spikes through both his shoulders, after tying his wrists behind his back with shrunken bits of rawhide.

He tried to move his arms and to roll onto his back. Nothing doing. He hadn't dreamt the part about his wrists being tied behind his back. And while he hadn't dreamt anything about his legs, his ankles were apparently trussed up behind his back as well. And secured to his wrists.

Hog-tied.

He snarled and fumed and gritted his teeth, lifting his head and arching his back to fight against his stays, until the forked veins in his forehead threatened to pop. But the more he struggled, the tighter the ropes seemed to become.

He looked around. Soft morning light lit the pines down the hill from the cave. The fire ring was heaped with white ashes. No sign of the girls.

His mind caught on the remembered image of Hank Maclean smoking his pipe. Had he dreamt that, or had Maclean really been here when Birt had bashed Longarm over the head with a rock just as he'd finished throwing the blocks to her sister?

Longarm saw the rock Birt had used, lying only a few feet away, near the pine boughs on which the girls had dried their clothes and upon which his clothes remained. Dried blood shone on the rock. It reminded Longarm that his head ached nearly as badly as his shoulders, which felt ready to pop from their sockets.

He ground his molars against his excruciating pain, and looked around once more for anything that might help to free him. Maclean must have tied him. He doubted either of the girls would have been strong enough to bind him this tightly.

So, the old man had been here . . .

Longarm wondered only vaguely what all this was about. All that concerned him now was getting free and getting dressed. Hog-tied naked after being seduced out of his wits . . .

Humiliation increased the burn in his joints and the throbbing pain in his head.

He flopped around, gritting his teeth as waves of agony rolled through him. On top of everything else, the morning was damn cold and, while his blankets were nearby, he had no way to roll up in them.

"Fuckin' bitches. Wait till I get my hands around both your scrawny necks!"

When he finally calmed himself down enough to think reasonably, he realized he needed something sharp. He found that something in a sharp-edged rock comprising the fire ring. Flopping toward the ring and wriggling around like a wounded snake, he managed to get his feet and wrists into position.

He started sawing. Then he started cursing. This was going to be no easy task. Nor a quick one. At least, as he worked in a fumbling, awkward manner against the rock, he warmed quickly, and sweat soon beaded his forehead.

Strand by strand, curse by curse, the rope gave.

Nearly a half hour after he'd started, his wrists parted and his feet flopped down to the cave floor. He groaned as those railroad spikes in his shoulders jerked and twisted, and he imagined he could hear those gnomes giggling again at their handiwork.

Longarm lay flat on his back staring at the sky, letting the pain in his body subside. He'd have the headache a good long time, judging from the amount of crusted blood on his forehead, cheek, and jaw.

He inspected the gash with his fingers. It wasn't long, but it was about a quarter-inch deep. Lucky he didn't bleed to death.

Lucky he had a damn thick skull . . .

Birt had drilled him good. Longarm chuckled without mirth, and rage seared him once more.

"Hold on, hoss," he told himself as he gained his bare feet and reached for his clothes. "Keep your wits. You ain't out of the woods yet. You better hope like hell they left you a horse."

He'd already spied his .44 still coiled where he'd reached for it when Randi had visited his night sack to fuck him and damn near kill him. But his rifle was gone. Maclean had likely taken it to replace his old Spencer. A quick peek into his vest pocket told him they'd left his double-barreled derringer as well.

"Well, I'm armed anyway," he muttered when he'd donned his dry clothes and stepped gently into his shrunken boots.

If they'd left him a horse, however, he'd be damn surprised. With a horse, he'd run them down. He'd run them down anyway, but they didn't know that. They probably figured he'd be so humiliated after being fucked, stoned, and hog-tied, that he'd slink on back to Denver with his tail between his legs.

"Nah, I'm not gonna do that," he said, staring into the trees down the slope from the cave, gritting his teeth against the blacksmith's hammer mercilessly bending nails against the inside of his skull. "I'm gonna find out what your game is. And if it ain't that fuckin' Silverjack loot those killers murdered Richard for, I'll be a monkey's uncle."

He hitched up his cartridge belt and his whipcord trousers, and started slowly down the muddy hill and into the softly dripping pines. He moved carefully, afraid of slipping and increasing his misery. Not surprised to find the horses missing from their picket line, he moved around the side of the slope for a time, whistling.

Nothing. The horses were gone. Likely, the mules were, too.

Finally, he continued to the bottom of the slope and

found the wagon still mired in the wash, the morning sun beating off its sodden canvas, which smelled like old tar. Murky water churned up around the Conestoga's wheel hubs.

A large plank and several freight items—picks, axes, and a couple of cases of flour and miners' heavy dungarees— lay in the dirty water at the edge of the bank.

Longarm climbed down into the creek, slogging through the gurgling, clay-colored water, and swept the rear pucker open with both hands. He looked into the back of the wagon, and froze.

There was a clear space where the supplies had been removed. At the rear of the clear space, inches from the open tailgate, a secret compartment had been exposed when the plank had been ripped away. The space beneath the wagon's floor, likely where tools had once been stored, was deep enough to hide a strongbox.

Longarm's heart quickened. He gritted his teeth against the increased throb in his head. He threw the pucker flaps back into place and wheeled angrily, cursing, bunching his lips, and shaking his head.

Those little bitches had been hauling the strongbox all along. And Longarm had been helping them!

The thuds of distant hooves sounded. He turned to see two riders galloping across the sage flat on the other side of the flooded wash—within two hundred yards and closing. He'd just wondered if they'd spied him here by the wagon, when one flung an arm out, pointing at him, and turned his head toward his partner. The man's voice reached Longarm's ears a full second later, though from this distance he couldn't hear the man's words.

They'd seen him, all right. And doubtless they were part

of the thieving, murdering gang on the scout for the stolen loot.

His heartbeat quickening, Longarm stared at the two men quirting their mounts with their rein ends, his eyes hooded and bright with harried thought.

He needed a horse. Well, here were two . . .

Not caring if the riders saw him now—in fact, hoping they saw every move he made—he exaggerated his movements as he splashed through the stream and scrambled up the bank. He paused for a stretched second to stare back at the two men who had their mounts stretched out in full gallops, angling toward him, sunlit dust rising behind them.

The rider on the left reached forward, shucked a rifle from his saddle boot, and cocked it one-handed.

They were within a hundred yards of Longarm and closing fast, the thuds of their horse's hooves growing louder.

Longarm touched his holstered .44 and yearned for his Winchester, with which he could have made fast work of the two men bearing down on him. But he only had the pistol, which meant he had to be creative . . .

Suppressing the pain in his joints and skull, he turned away from the wash and bolted into a dead run into the trees, making a show of casting fearful looks over his shoulder until he was angling up the slope and into the forest.

Shouts rose behind him. He smiled grimly and continued running, leaping deadfalls and meandering around boulders, gradually angling up the steepening ridge.

His energy was low, and he hadn't run far before he had to stop and catch his breath, continuing to shove the pain in his shoulders, hips, back, and head into a dark little pocket in his brain and close the lid on it.

Behind him, shouts rose. Fierce splashes sounded, then silence. He looked back through the trees but could make out only the wagon's sunlit canvas.

The riders were likely fording the stream.

Longarm looked around for cover. There was nothing but the scattered pines and aspens, with here and there a small, mossy boulder.

There was another splash behind him. Longarm's blood quickened again, and he took off running up across the shoulder of the slope.

Hoof thuds sounded, and twigs and branches snapped. A man shouted. A pistol popped. The slug slammed into an aspen trunk to Longarm's right.

He flinched and continued running, trying to zigzag now. The riders were close enough that he could hear their horses snorting and blowing.

"We got him on the run, Wade!" one of the pursuers cried.

Another pistol popped. The bullet whined over Longarm's head and blew up grass and pine needles twenty yards ahead. A rifle barked, and the slug broke a dead branch to Longarm's left before tearing bark from a pine bole just beyond it.

Longarm glanced over his right shoulder as he ran, his lungs feeling raw. He was losing the war with his misery, and his head ached so badly that his ears rang and his eyes watered. He felt the cool thickness of fresh blood pumping from the gash in his temple and dribbling down his cheek.

The riders were hammering toward him, about twenty yards apart, their horses leaping deadfalls and twisting around trees, both riders ducking under branches as their hat brims obscured their unshaven faces. As one horse leaped a lightning-felled aspen and hit the ground just beyond it, its rider—a big man in a bear coat—grunted loudly from the impact.

The man steadied his rifle over his chestnut's head. Orange flames licked from the maw. The whip-crack echoed around the trees. The slug nipped the shoulder nap of Longarm's frock and blasted a pine bole just beyond. The loud spang sounded like a rusty door hinge on Hell's gate.

Running, elbows sawing at his sides, breath whistling in and out of his lungs, Longarm swerved this way and that, raking his eyes around the terrain before him, looking for cover.

Nothing.

Then, twenty yards away, he spied a sunlit clearing. A boulder sat the middle of the clearing.

Behind him, one of the men whooped like a wolf on the blood scent. The pistol and the rifle exploded at nearly the same time. One of the bullets clipped Longarm's heel, nudging the boot to one side. He broke stride with a startled grunt, hit the ground, and rolled.

He was on his feet a half second later, bolting into the clearing, hearing the guns popping behind him, the horses pounding toward him, tack squawking, saddlebags flapping, bridle chains rattling.

The hunters were close enough for Longarm's Colt.

If he could get behind the boulder that was twenty yards ahead and leaping and jostling toward him with each of his harried strides, and get his feet solidly beneath him, the advantage would be his.

He dove as two more bullets screeched around him and blasted the boulder, flinging rock shards in all directions.

Hitting the ground beside the boulder, he rolled behind it.
He rose to a knee, his .44 in his right hand. He extended the
double-action Colt out and slightly up before him.

Both riders were within ten yards, one on either side of
the boulder. Longarm lined up his Colt's sights on the bear-
coated gent's chest. When the man saw the Colt bearing
down on him, his lower jaw dropped and his eyes widened.

He was levering a fresh round into his Winchester one-
handed when Longarm squeezed the Colt's trigger.

Pop!

"Oh!" the bear-coated gent cried.

He threw his rifle away as though it had suddenly become hot, and rolled straight back off his horse's rump,
turning a somersault in midair—an oddly graceful move for
one so large and unwieldy. He hit the ground with a crunching thump.

His black hat bounced straight up, the hammered silver
discs adorning the crown flashing in the sunlight.

As the man rolled, groaning, his horse continuing on
past Longarm, screaming, Longarm leaped behind the
boulder's right side. The other rider galloped past the opposite side, triggering his revolver twice, the slugs cutting the
air where Longarm had been a second ago, plunking into
the ground and blowing up rocks and sage branches.

Longarm bolted out from behind the rock and, crouching, triggered four quick shots as the rider galloped away.
For a second, Longarm thought he'd missed the man
cleanly, but then, when the man's bay was twenty yards
away from the boulder, heading toward the far side of the
clearing, the man slumped forward. As horse and rider
neared the trees, the man sagged down the left side of his
saddle.

A pine bole caught him, smacking him hard about the

head and shoulders with an audible thud. The bay continued into the trees as the rider pinwheeled wildly and hit the
ground belly down, limbs akimbo.

The dew-dappled grass waved around him.

He didn't move.

Chapter 17

Drunk with pain and stiffness, Longarm took nearly an hour to run down the outlaw's bay.

It was a surly horse anyway—Longarm could see the obstinate fire in its red brown eyes. And after the three slugs Longarm had pumped into its rider, with a fourth blazing a bloody swath across the mount's ass, the gelding was bound and determined to stand in a clearing down close to the flooded wash, nibbling fescue and and bunchgrass at its leisure and swishing its broom tail at flies.

Stubborn and owly though it was, the bay was not particularly bright, and it followed its graze right up against a low escarpment. Longarm worked around the horse, climbed the escarpment from the far side, and simply dropped down into the saddle.

After an excruciating couple of minutes of buck-kicking and sun-fishing during which the lawman thought his battered head was going to explode, he brought the horse back under its bit. Blowing horse and aching rider set off along the wash under a tense truce flag, following the two sets of mule tracks and the two sets of horse tracks that were several hours old and growing older.

Hank Maclean and the Lyndecker girls swerved left of the old stage road to Cimarron, and followed a meandering course due south through a broad valley between the Sangre de Cristos and the San Juan range. Longarm had no idea where they were headed—possibly toward Mexico, where they'd sell the gold across the border and come back rich—and he didn't care.

As long as he ran the fools down before the remaining four members of the gang did. As he rode, following the tracks, he had plenty of time to think, and he decided he'd secure the loot first, then see about hauling the other four killers to justice.

Justice.

Longarm smiled grimly. His kill fury had ebbed. It was probably Maclean himself who'd dampened the flames, throwing Longarm's lawless gun trail intentions up in front of the longtime lawman's face where he could get a good look at them and compare them to what his boss, Chief Marshal Billy Vail, would expect of him.

Yeah, he'd bring them to justice. Richard would be avenged. Whether Longarm could do it without having to beef the killers was a separate problem.

But arresting the men and hauling them back to a judge and jury was his intention now—not cold-blooded vengeance—and he marveled at how much better it made him feel inside.

"Billy, you old son of a bitch."

The red-eyed bay twitched its ears and glanced back at him.

"Wasn't talking to . . ."

Longarm let his voice trail off as he stared down at the ground. Suddenly, he hauled back on the bay's reins and stepped out of the saddle, wincing at the agonizing pain spasm ignited by the sudden movement.

Holding the reins in one hand, he dropped to a knee and ran a gloved hand across his cheek as he inspected the four sets of horse prints that intersected with the four he'd been following.

The new four came in from the direction of Cimarron.

Longarm's pulse quickened as he looked around, scouring the ground with his eyes, prodding a pile of horse apples with his boot toe. The four sets of relatively recent tracks didn't just intersect those of Maclean and the Lyndecker girls. They overlaid them.

Longarm looked south, the bay snorting and stomping behind him. His heart pumped faster. With a muttered curse, he swung up into the leather and booted the bay ahead along the tracks scoring the sage and bunchgrass flat.

The outlaws—and who else could the tracks belong to except for the Silverjack thieves?—were about two hours behind the old man and the girls, about three ahead of Longarm. If he didn't catch up to the girls and the old man first, he'd likely catch up to nothing but three crow-bait carcasses, with the gold and the last four killers lighting a shuck for Mexico.

He'd already run the horse plenty, but he ran him again.

Longarm wasn't sure from the tracks how quickly the four outlaws were catching up to Maclean and the girls. But by five o'clock that evening, as he rode over a saddleback ridge with thunder once again rumbling and distant lightning flashing, the bay gave a snort and shook its head.

Longarm stopped the horse just down from the ridge, and placed his hand on the stock of the Winchester snugged down in the saddle boot beneath his right thigh.

"What is it, boy?"

Longarm's respect for the horse had grown since finding out how well and how fast the animal could cover ground, and after it had warned Longarm of a small party of Ute warriors squatting around a cookfire in an adjacent valley several hours ago.

Now the lawman followed the bay's wary stare down the saddleback ridge toward a small grove of cottonwoods jutting from a green area around what was obviously a spring. He saw it then, too—something hanging from a branch of one of the cottonwoods.

The muscles at the small of Longarm's back tightened with dread as he kicked the bay down the ridge. The hanging figure before him jostled with the horse's pitch and sway. He drew closer until he could see the bearded features of Hank Maclean wrenched painfully in death as the rope around the man's grizzled neck twisted and creaked in the growing breeze.

The old man's hands had been tied behind his back. His cheeks were cut and bruised, and dried blood could be seen at the right corner of his mouth. His hat was gone, only the whites of his eyes appeared, and his thin, salt-and-pepper hair slid around his head. The toes of his worn, mule-eared boots traced lazy half circles in the air only two feet from the ground.

Likely, the killers had hanged him slowly, winching him up by small increments above the ground, until the old man had gradually, painfully strangled, probably jerking and kicking like a fish on a line.

Longarm chuffed air through his nose, grinding his teeth

at the killers' cruelty despite the old man's transgressions. He cut the body down and laid it out beneath the trees.

He wouldn't take the time to bury the man, for the killers had obviously taken the girls. There was no telling what manner of torment Randi and Birt were enduring at that very moment.

The fact that the girls were with the killers was poignantly evident when, filling his canteen at the spring, Longarm spied a bare footprint in the mud at the edge of the water, and the larger print of one spurred boot nearby.

He didn't know when the girls and their father, old Lin Lyndecker himself, had thrown in with the killers. They could have been in on the robbery from the beginning, or maybe they'd just been used to transport the strongbox after it had been stolen.

Still, Longarm felt no light worry pang for both girls, who'd likely become involved in something far bigger and more deadly than they'd realized, and something that had likely been initiated by their pugnacious old man.

Longarm had to overtake the killers before the girls ended up like Maclean.

He took a drink from the canteen and let the bay have his fill of the tooth-splintering cold springwater. Then, as the thunder continued to rumble in the gunmetal blue sky behind him, he looped the canteen over his saddle horn, stepped into the saddle, pulled the bay's head up from the water, and booted him up the trail.

The thunder continued to rumble for about an hour, but the storm, with its stacked, menacing, rain-swollen clouds, swerved northward. Longarm felt only a few chill raindrops against his back.

The wind was refreshingly cool, and it was in the cool of the storm-washed evening that, three hours after finding

Maclean's body, he crouched on the side of a sagey knoll
and stared into a narrow valley in which a lone cabin
hunched at the base of a pine-studded ridge. Smoke curled
from the cabin's tin chimney pipe, and in the covered corral
to the right of the cabin, several horses and two mules stood
in three stiff clumps, a couple of the horses lazily swishing
their tails.

An eerie silence hung over the valley. The four men and
the girls were probably in the cabin, from which no sounds
emanated.

Longarm was a good hundred yards away from the
cabin's front door, and all he could hear was the creek
chuckling through wolf willows behind him, and the lonesome bird calls on the piney ridges. The eastern ridge was
nearly crimson with late light; the western ridge over Longarm's right shoulder was purple with cool, fast-thickening
shadows.

There wasn't a breath of wind.

On this high shoulder of the San Juan Range, it was getting cold fast. Longarm wished he had his coat. He raked a
thumbnail along his unshaven jaw as he studied the cabin.
He had a feeling he'd warm up soon—when he figured out
what play he was going to make to save the girls and re-
cover the loot.

If the girls needed saving, that is. It had occurred to him
that, as frisky as Birt and Randi were, they might have
made some kind of arrangement to throw in with the four
killers. A small cut of the loot was better than no cut at
all . . . and cut throats.

Longarm glanced behind him. The bay had settled
down—worn out mostly from the long, hard pull. It stood
tied to a lone cedar in the green willows along the creek,

idly cropping needle grass, blocked from view from the cabin by Longarm's knoll.

After a careful scrutiny of the area around the cabin, he stole down from the knoll to the bay. He'd slipped the horse's bit so it could forage, and now he unbuckled its belly strap as well.

He shucked the Winchester carbine from the saddle boot, ran a thoughtful hand down the forestock. He didn't like using a gun he wasn't familiar with, because each one had its own personality. But any rifle was better than no rifle. He might not get close enough to use his revolver, and if they got him pinned down somewhere outside of the cabin with only the Colt, he'd be wolf bait by midnight.

After making sure both weapons were loaded, he spun the Colt's cylinder, dropped the iron into its cross-draw holster, and snapped the keeper thong over the hammer. He kept his head down as he ran straight west of the bay, who watched him curiously as he disappeared into the wolf willows and potentillas.

He followed the heavy growth of the stream up past the cabin, then left the creek and climbed the steep, pine-studded ridge directly behind the hovel—which appeared to be an abandoned line shack.

On the slope of the ridge facing the cabin, he hunkered down, made sure no one was out in the yard, then stole down the slope, sidestepping so he didn't fall and injure himself further. His shoulders were still stiff and sore, and his head still ached, though not as badly as before.

As he gained the slope's bottom and started through the scrub brush toward the cabin's rear wall, where there was one curtained window but no door, a girl's screech sounded. Longarm stepped behind the plank-board, tin-roofed privy and felt his finger tighten against the Winchester's curved trigger, his gloved thumb caressing the hammer.

"Son of a bitch!" Birt cried.

She said something else, her voice raised indignantly, but Longarm couldn't make out the words.

A man laughed. Then there was the clatter of a tin cup probably thrown against a stout log wall.

Longarm licked his lower lip. The gang had the girls all right. And Birt, at least, was still kicking. Now, to get her and her sister out of the cabin without getting them killed . . .

The lawman moved forward, stepping around sage shrubs and skirting a timbered root cellar built low to the ground, until he'd gained the cabin's rear wall, right of the window, which was obscured by a tattered flour-sack curtain.

Pressing his ears to the mud-chinked logs, he could hear faint voices inside. Mostly men's voices, but a couple of times he thought he heard Randi's voice as well.

There were light ticking sounds, as though pasteboards were being snapped down against a wooden table.

Someone was playing poker.

Longarm crept around the cabin's rear corner and started up its north side toward the front. He'd thought, when scrutinizing the cabin from the knoll, that the front door had been partly open. That would be the way he'd go in then. Hopefully, he'd take the gang by surprise and they'd give themselves up instead of opting for a lead swap. In such close quarters, a shoot-out would likely result in the girls taking bullets.

He didn't know why he gave a damn—after Randi had soundly used her lusty wares to trick him, and Birt had nearly cracked his skull with the stone—but, to his chagrin, he did.

Longarm stepped up to the lone window on the north side of the cabin. He shallowed his breath and listened, hearing a man say tauntingly, "... not gonna get you and li'l sis out of this sitchy-ation that way, Miss Randi. My queen beats your sixes. You mighta started out right lucky, but your cards are comin' up *low!*"

The man chuckled eagerly.

"Ow!" That was Birt from the back of the cabin. "Quit bitin' my neck, you plug-ugly bastard!"

"Ah, come on—give me some sugar, sweetie!" a man beseeched.

"You're ugly and you smell!" Birt scolded.

Several other men laughed.

"Hold on, Birt," Randi said as the cards were being shuffled. "I'll get us outta here with this next hand. I'm feelin' lucky!"

Longarm wasn't overly confident that the pretty brunette was going to win her and her sister's freedom anytime soon. He was about to duck under the window and continue to the front of the cabin, when Birt said, "You bite my neck once more, you son of a bitch, I'm gonna scream so loud my lawdog friend, Custis P. Long his ownself, hears and comes runnin'. He's probably broke loose from his ties and is trackin' us right now. In fact, he's probably right outside waitin' to shoot your ugly eyes out!"

Longarm crouched low against the base of the cabin, silently sucking air through his teeth and grimacing.

"Longarm?" one of the men said, concern in his voice.

"That's right!" Birt challenged.

"Shit," Longarm breathed, pressing his back against the cabin's rough timbers. "Shit, shit, shit!"

One of the men chuckled. "She's been reading too many dime novels, Red."

"Just in case," Red said, "one o' you boys go out and walk around. Surtees, you go. You got the best eyes and ears. Besides, the others been drinkin'."

Longarm's heart thudded as a deep voice—probably belonging to Surtees—muttered a curse and spat. A chair raked loudly across uneven floor puncheons. Boots clomped and spurs chinged. There was the rattle of a belt buckle.

Longarm looked around for a place to hide, grumbling, "Thanks, Birt. 'Preciate that . . ."

Nothing around him but sage and occasional stunt cedars, rocks no larger than washtubs, and bunchgrass clumps. As the men continued conversing inside the cabin, and the boots continued to scuff, Longarm looked beyond the cabin's rear.

The ridge rose sixty yards out, and the pines along the slope didn't start until another forty yards from the base. No way Longarm could reach them before Surtees spied him. He glanced at the root cellar and, as the front door of the cabin squawked open, he started for it, hoping the cellar door opened easily and that there was room for a man to crouch inside.

He could stay out here and take Surtees down easily with the Winchester, but then the others would pour out of the cabin, likely surround him, and turn him into a human sieve before he could get more than maybe one of the three.

He bolted out from the side of the cabin, and stopped.

He swung his head toward a woodpile abutting the cabin's rear wall, on the other side of the single window.

He looked from the woodpile to the roof—an easy climb—and arched a brow. At the same time, Surtees's footsteps sounded along the side of the cabin, growing louder.

Chapter 18

The boot thuds and spur chings grew louder as Longarm quickly but quietly climbed atop the woodpile. He started to reach for the ceiling overhang, and pulled his arms back down suddenly.

Surtees was almost to the corner.

Longarm's pulse hammered. On one knee atop the gray logs, he swung his carbine toward the cabin corner, and ratcheted back the hammer. He brought the butt to his shoulder.

The killer's tall, slender shadow stretched out from behind the side of the cabin, lying flat atop the silver green sage and coarse gravel that had turned gray as the sun sank behind the mountains. As the shadow slid along the ground, Longarm slowly took up the slack in the trigger. Then he gave it some slack and frowned down the Winchester's barrel.

Surtees's shadow came no farther.

Then Longarm saw part of a shoulder slide out from the cabin corner, and heard a match strike to life. The edge of a black hat brim and a black-clad elbow could be seen as

Surtees swung around to face away from the cabin. Smoke wafted on the still air as the killer fired a cigarette.

Quickly, Longarm depressed the carbine's hammer and, nervously stretching his lips back from his teeth, slid the carbine atop the shake-shingled roof. He grabbed the edge of the roof with both hands, and prayed the ceiling wouldn't creak and groan as he hoisted himself up.

He'd no sooner settled his knee atop the cabin and grabbed his Winchester, than he saw Surtees stroll out from around the side of the cabin, the quirley jutting from beneath his thickly mustached lip, and move out behind the hovel, hitching his pants up with one hand and holding his Sharps carbine across his shoulder with the other.

The man moved to near where Longarm had been standing a minute ago, and from above, the black hat brim now covered his face and cigarette. As the man stopped to look around behind the cabin, sighing and blowing smoke out from beneath the black hat brim, Longarm leaned far back away from the roof edge. He could no longer see the man, but he listened to him kicking around the cabin for about five more minutes before Surtees went inside and closed the door.

Longarm could hear muffled conversation beneath him.

He had started to climb back down toward the edge of the roof, when he glanced at the chimney pipe and froze. A minute ago, he'd heard the squawk of the stove door, and a thump as someone chunked more wood onto the fire.

Thick smoke billowed from the chimney pipe, wafting on the fast-darkening air.

Up near the base of the pipe lay a stick with burlap wrapped and tied around one end. The stick was used to plug up the chimney when no one was here, to prevent birds from building nests inside.

Longarm looked at the stick, then at the pipe, and a cunning light entered his eyes. If he could smoke the rats out of their hole, and bear down on them with the carbine from over the door, he'd have them dead to rights.

Longarm crawled slowly—moving one limb at a time and gritting his teeth at the squawk and creak in the shingles beneath him—toward the chimney pipe. He picked up the stick, rose slowly onto his knees, straightening his back, and stuffed the burlap end of the stick into the mouth of the pipe.

He waited, listening.

Someone coughed. Someone else coughed. One of the girls complained. Longarm smiled. Smoke was pushing out of the stove door and into the cabin.

Grinning, he grabbed his rifle and began crawling toward the front of the cabin. Beneath him, the roof creaked menacingly. There was a snap like that of a twig breaking.

He froze, looked down at the gray, rotten shakes beneath him. A cold stone dropped in his belly. His eyes grew wide. He moved his left hand forward.

The roof dropped several inches beneath him with another tooth-gnashing cracking sound.

"Ah, no!"

He tried to scramble forward and away from the rotten area, but he hadn't made it six inches before the roof groaned, creaked, cracked, and crunched, and he found himself falling back and down amidst breaking shingles and ceiling timbers, into a smoky, gauzy world of darkness where the smell of fried side pork registered dimly on his consciousness.

A man shouted.

A girl screamed.

Another girl screamed.

Something hard came up beneath Longarm and smacked his butt and the backs of his legs. He plowed right through the table.

Something harder and less yielding and that could only have been the floor came up to smack him even harder, causing those pain bells in his skull, which had quieted considerably, to start ringing again in earnest.

As the floor slammed up against his back and the back of his head, laying him out flat though he was somehow still clinging to the carbine, he heard the breath leave his lungs in a loud *whooosh!*

Around him, people coughed raucously. Boots pounded the floor, causing the boards beneath Longarm to leap and shudder.

"What the *fuck*?" a man shouted.

"The door, you stupid fucker!" yelled another man somewhere on the floor to Longarm's right. His voice was pinched with pain, and Longarm figured he must have struck the curly wolf when he'd come through the ceiling. "Open the fucking door! We got company—*cough! cough!*—and it ain't Santy Claus!"

Amidst more yells—the girls' as well as the men's—Longarm heard the door open. From somewhere on the other side of the roof debris, a pistol popped. The slug slammed into the log wall behind Longarm.

Vaguely surprised to find no bones broken—at least not in his arms and chest, though his shoulders were throbbing nearly as badly as his head—Longarm aimed the Winchester across his chest. He fired at the spot where he'd glimpsed the pistol flash.

More shouts and boot thuds. The scrape of chairs and tables rose from the gauzy, billowing smoke. A bottle shattered on the floor. Someone ratcheted a gun hammer back, lifting the hair on the back of Longarm's neck.

He pushed up onto his knees and blinked against the smoke that stung his eyes and increased the throbbing in his head. Tears streamed down his cheeks. He tried to speak, only inhaled a mouthful of smoke, and choked.

"Longarm—deputy U.S. marshal!" he finally managed in a pinched shout, his lungs and throat contracting. "Throw down your irons, you stupid sonso'bitches!"

"The girl was tellin' it straight!" a man shouted.

"Fuckin' law!"

From the front of the cabin, two pistols popped. The slugs screeched around Longarm, one plunking a wall far wide of him, the other hammering a stout ceiling joist three feet to his right, making a hanging lantern clang. Longarm returned fire, hoping the girls were either outside or on the floor, cowering under a cot or a table.

A sharp curse and a shrill grunt sounded from the billowing smoke curtain where Longarm had sent the two .44 slugs. A revolver roared behind him and to the right. The bullet whined past the end of his nose and shattered the cabin's east window.

Longarm swung around and, jacking and levering the carbine from his hip, emptied the rifle at a vague figure appearing and disappearing behind the billowing smoke curtain. Before the carbine's echoes had died, he was rewarded with a shrill curse and the loud, resounding thump of a body hitting the floor.

He looked around, but the smoke gushing from the open door of the potbelly stove crouched on the other side of the room was as thick as snow in a Dakota blizzard. He tossed away the carbine, palmed his pistol, and holding a flap of his coat up over his mouth and nose, scrambled toward the door. He kicked a couple of chairs and a table leg, sent a bottle spinning across the floorboards.

Making the door, beyond which he could hear a couple of men and the girls coughing and cursing, he cocked the Colt and bolted outside, swerving sharply left. He cleared the smoke emanating from the door, and saw through his watery, stinging eyes the girls and two men. One man was down on a knee, his thick gray hair flopping down over his forehead as he hunkered low, coughing his lungs out.

The other, bent forward, coughing and dabbing at his eyes with his red neckerchief, glanced up at Longarm. His eyes snapping wide, he straightened and jerked up a long-barreled, silver-plated Remington that he'd been holding in his right hand.

Before he could get a shot off, Longarm aimed hastily, the man's image quavering and wavering before his tear-burning eyes, and fired twice. As the man grunted and stumbled straight backward, sending a bullet screaming toward the cabin's roof, the other gent reached for a rifle lying in the sage by his left boot.

"Think again, hombre!" Longarm shouted.

The man only bellowed and grabbed the gun.

Longarm fired once, but just then he had to squeeze his eyes closed against the searing smoke burn. He felt as though someone had flung red pepper into both eyes.

Trying to open his lids as tears gushed down his cheeks, soaking his mustache, he fired three more rounds quickly as he watched the gray-haired gent aim his Winchester at him.

The rifle exploded, the slug whipping over Longarm's left shoulder to bark off a rock somewhere behind him.

Longarm peeled one aching, burning eyelid open, drew

a bead on the man's chest as the man quickly racked another round into his Winchester's breech, and fired.

Dust puffed from the middle of the man's dark blue, bib-front shirt. His red neckerchief billowed as the heart shot punched the man back and twisted him around.

He fired his Winchester through the toe of his left boot. Screaming shrilly, he hopped once, then fell in a bloody heap on his back, his arms and legs and bloody boot twitching as though he were trying to become airborne.

A gun roared to Longarm's right, the red flames flashing amidst the smoke still pouring out the door. Longarm wheeled and fired into the smoke. At the same time, a stocky figure dropped to his knees just outside the door, and Longarm's bullet whipped through the open door behind him and crunched into a wall or ceiling joist inside.

The man pushed himself up and forward, stumbling out away from the cabin. Longarm aimed and triggered the Colt once more. His loins turned cold as the hammer clicked against the firing pin—empty.

The stocky gent walked toward Longarm, raising the old Schofield in his left fist, his long, green neckerchief billowing in the chill night breeze. He coughed a couple of times, but continued toward Longarm, blinking against the tears dribbling down his ruddy cheeks, his lips stretched back from three or four chipped, cracked teeth remaining in his tobacco brown jaws.

A long, brown mustache drooped down over both corners of his mouth, and his red brown hair was cropped close to his head. His eyes flashed in the twilight—cobalt blue and flat with deadly menace.

"You son of a bitch." He laughed. "You done left me with all the loot. Fuck, I should buy ya a drink as shoot ya!"

"Sounds good to me." Lowering his Colt to his side, Longarm watched the black ring of the Schofield's maw bear down on him, aimed at his forehead.

When the gun was two feet away from Longarm's face, the man stopped and scowled. "What's a federal lawman trackin' us fer anyways?"

"You killed a good friend of mine," Longarm bit out, bunching his lips with barely controlled rage. "I set out to kill every one of you louse-ridden coyotes, to settle up for a man who couldn't do it himself. Richard Collins. Remember that name. 'Cause when you go knocking on the Pearly Gates—you stinking dung beetle!—St. Pete's gonna say it one more time, to remind you. And you're gonna hear me and ole Richard laughing and clinking our shot glasses behind him as he sends you to the burning tar pits."

"Yeah?" The stocky, blue-eyed gent spat. "Laugh at this, Lawdog!"

POW!

Longarm closed his eyes and winced.

POW! POW! POW!

Longarm opened his eyes, heart hammering, frowning curiously.

The blue-eyed gent stood before him, swaying like a windmill in a cyclone. He stared at Longarm. He opened his mouth as though to speak, and a thick gob of blood ran down over his bottom lip.

Then Longarm saw the two blood-pumping holes in the man's pin-striped shirt, and another in his left cheek.

"Oh," the man said, stumbling sideways like a drunk about to pass out, slightly amused by his condition. "Shit on a shingle . . . !"

Then he stumbled and fell in a heap, smashing his own gun against his jaw with an audible smack.

Longarm looked through the curls of smoke wisping ten yards straight out from the cabin door before licking skyward. Birt and Randi were kneeling in the yard near the two men Longarm had beefed when he'd first bolted from the shack. Randi was down on all fours, looking up at Longarm, shock in her eyes.

Birt knelt several yards to the left of her sister, holding a pearl-gripped Smith & Wesson in both her hands, which appeared terribly small and delicate against the heavy, iron weapon. Smoke curled from the Smithy's barrel as Birt slowly lowered it to the ground between her knees.

A gleeful glitter shone in her eyes. She looked from the dead, blue-eyed gent whom she'd killed to Longarm, as though searching for his approval. The lawman ran a hand across his chin, holstered his .44, and strode toward the blonde, regarding her grimly.

Randi looked at Birt. "The strongbox," she muttered, as though half to herself. "That loot could be ours, Sister."

She glanced pensively at Longarm, her brown eyes flashing with greed. "*All* ours."

Longarm looked at Birt. The blonde was staring at him. Lines etched themselves across Birt's forehead. Quickly, she glanced down at the still-smoking Smithy. She glanced up at Longarm again as he drew to within three feet and stopped, looking down at her.

Birt tossed the Smithy into the brush.

Randi lowered her head with a groan.

"How long you had the loot?" Longarm asked, his voice taut and even, deep-pitched with contempt.

A tear rolled out from Birt's left eye and dribbled down her smoothly rounded cheek. "A few hours out of Grand View. The gang stopped us, offered Pa five hundred dollars to deliver it to Cimarron."

"They figured a posse would overrun 'em," Longarm
said mostly to himself. "Figured they had to split up.
They'd move faster without the strongbox. And who'd sus-
pect two pretty girls and a Dakota farmer?"

"Then some decided to double back and take it all for
themselves," Birt said, sniffing and running the back of her
hand across her lightly freckled nose. "The others either got
wind of it or got the same idea."

"No honor among thieves," Longarm grunted. "How'd
Maclean figure in?"

Randi sighed and, rising to her knees, crossed her arms
on her chest. "He heard the two outlaws you beefed in
the roadhouse talking, found out about the loot in our
wagon."

"So, while I was out scouting around looking for Utes,
you three made a deal."

Randi nodded. "He said he'd tell you about the money
unless we let him in. He convinced us we could split it all
three ways and head to Arizona"—she dropped her head
guiltily—"once we were rid of you."

Longarm snorted and fingered the nasty gash on his
forehead. "Now, tell me—what am I gonna do with you
two? Prison's a hard place for girls."

The girls snapped horrified looks at him, and beseeched
at the same time, "Oh, please don't send us to prison!"

Randi alone said, "We didn't let old Maclean kill you
like he wanted, and we left your Colt!"

"Those men killed a good friend of mine," Longarm
said. "They killed several others, too. And then you damn
near helped 'em get away with the loot . . . not to mention
trying to steal the whole damn box for yourselves! It isn't
right I should let you go."

They both crawled on hands and knees toward Longarm, fear and desperation in their eyes.

"Please, Lawdog!" Birt cried. "We'll do *anything* to stay out of prison!"

"That's right," Randi said from down around Longarm's knees. *"Anything!"*

Longarm looked from one girl to the other. Then he looked off. "I can't just let you go. You need to be punished. You need to know that what you did was wrong. Dead wrong."

"You could whip us," Birt said. "That's what Pa done when we were bad."

Longarm considered it. He looked at Randi. "Go out there to those willows and find a good switch. I mean a *good* one. You bring me back some limp little thing, I'll haul you both back to Grand View for trial."

When Randi had brought back a suitable switch, and even skimmed all the leaves off it, Longarm whipped it across his palm several times. Deeming it sound, he looked around for the girls.

They were both leaning forward, their hands on a large rock, looking expectantly toward Longarm. Randi had her jeans and bloomers bunched around her ankles. Birt had raised her dress up across her back.

The girls' round, pink asses were visible in the gloaming—firm and tender and aimed at the sky.

"All right, Lawdog," Randi said, swallowing. "We're ready. Ain't we, Sis?"

Birt nodded eagerly. "Anything to stay out of the hot box!"

Longarm stared at the two pink rumps. The last light spread a salmon sheen across the smooth, round globe of each. Longarm's legs quivered slightly, and his loins grew warm and heavy.

None of this was really their fault. It was their cruel, old father's fault. Besides, they'd been punished enough.

What would Richard want him to do?

Longarm looked at those tender asses once more.

"Ah, Christ!" Flipping the switch over his shoulder, he headed off to fetch his horse.

Watch for

LONGARM AND THE GILA RIVER MURDERS

the 369ᵗʰ novel in the exciting LONGARM
series from Jove

Coming in August!

GIANT-SIZED ADVENTURE FROM
AVENGING ANGEL LONGARM.

BY TABOR EVANS

2006 Giant Edition:

LONGARM AND THE
OUTLAW EMPRESS

2007 Giant Edition:

LONGARM AND THE
GOLDEN EAGLE SHOOT-OUT

2008 Giant Edition:

LONGARM AND THE
VALLEY OF SKULLS

DON'T MISS A YEAR OF

Slocum Giant
by
Jake Logan

penguin.com/actionwesterns

M230AS0808

Penguin Group (USA) Online

What will you be reading tomorrow?

Tom Clancy, Patricia Cornwell, W.E.B. Griffin,
Nora Roberts, William Gibson, Robin Cook,
Brian Jacques, Catherine Coulter, Stephen King,
Dean Koontz, Ken Follett, Clive Cussler,
Eric Jerome Dickey, John Sandford,
Terry McMillan, Sue Monk Kidd, Amy Tan,
John Berendt…

You'll find them all at
penguin.com

***Read excerpts and newsletters,
find tour schedules and reading group guides,
and enter contests.***

Subscribe to Penguin Group (USA) newsletters
and get an exclusive inside look
at exciting new titles and the authors you love
long before everyone else does.

PENGUIN GROUP (USA)
us.penguingroup.com

M224G11107